D0210735

confessions of a
teen nanny

juicy secrets

A Novel by Victoria Ashton

⊽HarperTempest
An Imprint of HarperCollins*Publishers*
A PARACHUTE PRESS BOOK

Confessions of a Teen Nanny: Juicy Secrets
Copyright © 2006 by Parachute Publishing, L.L.C.
All rights reserved. No part of this book may be used or reproduced in any manner
whatsoever without written permission except in the case of brief quotations embodied
in critical articles and reviews. Printed in the United States of America. For information
address HarperCollins Children's Books, a division of HarperCollins Publishers, 1350
Avenue of the Americas, New York, NY 10019.

Library of Congress Cataloging-in-Publication Data

Ashton, Victoria.
Juicy secrets: a novel / by Victoria Ashton.— 1st ed.
p. cm.—(Confessions of a teen nanny; #3)
"A Parachute Press Book."
Summary: Two teen nannies become even more involved in the treacherous
world of their wealthy, elite employers as Adrienne begins a surprising new
relationship and Liz struggles to keep hers from falling apart.
ISBN-10: 0-06-073181-8 (trade bdg. : alk. paper)
ISBN-13: 978-0-06-073181-6 (trade bdg. : alk. paper)
ISBN-10: 0-06-077526-2 (lib. bdg. : alk. paper)
ISBN-13: 978-0-06-077526-1 (lib. bdg. : alk. paper)
[1. Nannies—Fiction. 2. Wealth—Fiction. 3. Dating (Social customs)—Fiction.
4. New York (N.Y.)—Fiction.] I. Title.
PZ7.A8295Jui 2006
[Fic]—dc22

2006000478

CIP
AC

❖

1 2 3 4 5 6 7 8 9 10

First Edition

To MFD—
the first boy I kissed and meant it

Contents

CHAPTER ONE

frozen hot gossip

"Did you know that if you grind up a tiger's hairs into a powder and give them to someone in a drink, they'll die a slow, painful death of internal bleeding from undetectable lacerations?" eight-year-old Emma Warner asked Adrienne Lewis as they walked hand-in-hand through Central Park.

"Emma, that is *so* gross," Adrienne said. "*Please* don't mention it over lunch with Liz, Heather, and David."

"Your endless capacity to avoid even the most basic confrontation never ceases to amuse me." Emma sighed. "Another piece of evidence."

Adrienne rolled her eyes. Even though Emma was off-the-charts smart for her age, she still could be a huge pain.

Adrienne looked across the broad expanse of Central Park, searching for her best friend on earth, Liz Braun.

Liz and Adrienne had been friends since the second grade, and only since high school had they been separated

1

for more than twelve minutes each day. With their mobiles and BlackBerries, the two girls were still inseparable—at least electronically. The one thing that brought them together face-to-face every day was the fact that they were both employed in the same building as nannies.

841 Fifth Avenue.

One of the legendary buildings in New York. The apartments started at $30 million, *and* you had to have ten times that in the bank to be accepted. The building was full of the city's elite—most importantly, Adrienne's and Liz's employers.

While Liz worked for Dr. Mayra Markham-Collins (known as Dr. M-C to the girls), a popular psychologist for children who made Dr. Phil look like a second-rate veterinarian, Adrienne worked for Catherine Olivia Warner (the COW), one of New York City's most prominent socialites. The girls had spent the past year caught in the whirlwind of the lives of their bosses: expensive trips to Palm Beach and Aspen, parties with the rich and decadent, and long, long days with their totally warped offspring. The rich *were* different, the girls had realized, but as long as they were paying, and paying big, why not enjoy the ride?

Adrienne waved at Liz and the two kids she took care of: David and Heather. David was adorable, Adrienne thought. A funny, sensitive five-year-old with an active imagination. Heather? Well, nine-year-old Heather was just sensitive and not particularly active.

"Hey, there!" Liz said, releasing David's hand for a second to wave to Adrienne. David bolted and ran to Adrienne, throwing his arms around her legs.

"Adrienne!" he shouted with glee. "Give me a cookie!"

Adrienne smiled. "I don't have a cookie, David. I'm a nanny, not a supermarket."

David let go and stared at her skeptically. "I bet you do," he said. "You're just mean." His face screwed up with tears.

"This is his new trick," Liz explained. "He learned it from Heather."

"Aha! Classic! David uses trust and affection to manipulate the subject," Emma said, taking out a small red leather notebook from her jacket pocket. "Then he makes an unusual request, causing the subject to feel as if she would be denying him her affection by refusing his request. That is the hallmark of the manipulative sociopath." She scribbled furiously. "Watch him, Liz," she said, closing the Smythson notebook that read EVIDENCE on the front cover. "He could be a budding serial killer."

"Well," Liz replied, "we know he'd kill for cereal!" She grinned. David's affection for junk food was well known, even though his mother refused to allow him to eat anything other than soy products. "Emma," Liz added, "what are you writing?"

"This is my evidence journal," Emma explained. "I keep track of everything now."

"Did Oprah tell you to do this?" Adrienne asked. Emma was completely obsessed with Oprah.

"Who watches *Oprah* anymore?" Emma sneered. "I am a devotee of *CSI*."

"Since when?"

"Since I grew up."

"I see." Adrienne raised an eyebrow, as Emma stashed her notebook in her coat pocket.

Liz and Adrienne watched the kids amble just ahead of them as they left the park and crossed Fifth Avenue.

Walking over to Lexington, the group made their way to Serendipity 3, the fabulous hangout near Bloomingdale's, famous for its frozen hot chocolate. An old soda fountain and gift shop, Serendipity was the cool place for kids to go during a day of shopping on Manhattan's Upper East Side. Its frozen hot chocolate was a New York institution.

"Hi there, Emma," chirped the man behind the reservation desk. Emma Warner, although only eight, was recognized throughout much of the Upper East Side.

"Hi, Reed," Emma said. "We want the downstairs corner booth."

"Kelli Huntington just sat there," Reed said. "I'm sorry."

Heather turned to Liz with fear in her eyes. "Don't

make me go in," she begged. "I *hate* Kelli Huntington."

"But, Heather—" Liz started.

"I would like to sit at my regular table, Reed," Emma continued. "Ask Kelli to move."

"Emma, I really can't—"

"Reed," Emma explained in a condescending tone Adrienne had heard Emma's mother use many times before. "I have a birthday party every year. I have one hundred kids. If I decide to have my party at your restaurant this year, that would be an awful lot of frozen hot chocolates. . . ." She smiled patiently.

"We do have a bigger table upstairs where the Huntingtons might be more comfortable," Reed said, knowing when he was beaten. The Warner money always won out.

"Thank you, Reed," Emma said, smiling sweetly.

"Thanks, Emma," Heather whispered, obviously relieved.

"Do you sometimes think that we nanny for Martians?" Adrienne asked, as the five kids slipped into "Emma's table" in the rear of the downstairs dining room, under a low-hanging Tiffany lamp.

"They're definitely different," Liz admitted, picking up a menu though knowing that they would all have foot-long hot dogs and frozen hot chocolate. When the frozen hot chocolates arrived, everyone plunged in with the long straws.

"That was a great party Tamara had," Liz said to Adrienne. "Too bad there isn't another party this weekend!"

"You got that right," Adrienne said. Last Saturday, Adrienne and her pals had partied long into the night with wild dancing and massive amounts of takeout food at Tamara Tucker's apartment on the Upper West Side. It was the first time since their breakup that Adrienne had seen her ex-boyfriend Brian Grady outside of school. What had made it even more significant was that the party had a Valentine's Day theme—Adrienne's first Valentine's Day solo in two years. At first she'd been afraid she'd get all weepy, but instead she had laughed, danced, and scarfed down delicious veggie dumplings. "That party rocked."

"For you," Liz said, giggling. "I don't think it was so cool for Brian. He was totally mooning over you."

Adrienne grinned. "So you noticed, too?"

"Please. He may have dumped you first, but now the tables are seriously turned."

"No joke," Adrienne agreed. "I never thought it was possible, but I really am so totally over him."

One month ago, Adrienne would never have been able to even imagine feeling this way. That was when her boyfriend of two years had dumped her for the glamorous celebutante Cameron Warner—Emma's seventeen-year-old half sister. Adrienne was shocked, hurt, and humiliated.

"It's great to hear you say that," Liz said. "I was pretty worried about you there for a while."

"Me, too," Adrienne admitted. "But I'm great now. No guys stressing me out." She glanced over at Emma, Heather, and David. They were all busy with the markers and paper Liz had brought with her. "How's Parker doing?" Adrienne asked her friend quietly.

Liz shrugged.

Parker Devlin and Liz had been seeing each other for a few months, and Adrienne had never seen Liz go for a guy the way she was gone over Parker.

"What happened?" Adrienne asked. "You have that look again. Whenever you scrunch up your face, I know you're upset."

"Nothing. Nothing happened," Liz confided. "I guess that's the problem. With Parker, it's hard to tell where things stand. It's just that he hasn't been around much this week. And he wouldn't come to Tamara's party with me."

"Maybe he's busy with school," Adrienne suggested, although she seriously doubted that was the case.

"Probably. But Parker is always busy with something. We have these really great dates—and then he drops off the planet for several days. I mean, don't you think he'd want to spend his time with *me*?" Liz said. "I want to spend *all* my time with him. He's so hot!"

"Guys are totally different from us," Adrienne said.

Liz nodded. "And rich guys are *way* different. Parker and Cameron aren't like normal kids."

Adrienne nodded. She had learned that the hard way, becoming friends with Cameron Warner. Cameron was Satan in a Dolce & Gabbana skirt. In her sixteen years growing up in New York City, Adrienne had never met anyone as manipulative and evil as Cameron.

"You should talk to Parker. Find out what's up with him," Adrienne told her friend.

"I couldn't do that," Liz said. "He'd freak."

"What then?" Adrienne asked. She slurped the last of the massive frozen chocolate drink.

"I guess I'll deal with the agony of not knowing what my boyfriend is up to the only way I know how." Liz's eyes twinkled mischievously.

Adrienne laughed and signaled the waiter over. "My friend needs a hot fudge sundae. Low on the ice cream, high on the hot fudge. We need emergency chocolate therapy here!"

CHAPTER TWO

back in the saddle

*C*rash!

The next afternoon, Liz Braun jumped at the sound of something large falling in the kitchen of Dr. Markham–Collins's ultramodern apartment. She quickly stepped out of the way as Heather raced from the kitchen.

"I didn't do it!" Heather shouted as she dashed past Liz down the hall.

Liz hurried into the kitchen to assess the damage. A toppled trash can lay on its side, and it had knocked over the bottle recycling bin. Organic fruit and vegetable juice bottles rolled around on the floor. Other than that, the room was empty.

"You didn't *mean* to do it, Heather," Liz called loudly, "but you *did* do it."

Liz sighed and tossed the bottles back into the blue bin, then re-righted the trash can. "I thought I was the nanny, not the housekeeper," she muttered.

As she gathered up spilled garbage, she noticed a pile of mail mixed in with the limp sprouts and soy-carob brownie wrappers.

"These should go in the paper bin," she muttered. Liz plucked out the mail—all brochures, she noted—trying to figure out how they had all wound up in the wrong bin. Dr. Markham-Collins was a recycling maniac.

She glanced at the brochures: STAGECRAFT MANOR, Liz read. THEATER CAMP FOR THE SHY AND RECLUSIVE CHILD. CAMP BUCK-EM-UP. DAY CAMP FOR THE DEPRESSED PRETEEN. Liz shook her head. *Poor Heather!* she thought. *She's not the most confident kid, but honestly! "Camp Buck-em-up"?*

No wonder Heather had tossed this stuff in the garbage—it's where crap like it belongs. The camps sounded like the Sixth Level of Hell for Heather, who was shy and nervous on her best days. Dr. Markham-Collins, Heather's overbearing and social-climbing mother, had just made things worse. For a woman who made her living by understanding and helping children, Dr. M-C was totally clueless when it came to her own.

Liz dumped the mail back into the trash. *We'll let this one slide,* she thought, tipping the trash can so that the brochures dropped down toward the bottom.

Suddenly the kitchen doors flung open, and Dr. Markham-Collins appeared framed in the doorway.

Everything about her was larger than life. She was almost six feet tall, and today her unruly dark hair was held on top of her head by a series of children's colored pencils. Her signature black-rimmed glasses were tucked in her capacious bosom, and a fuchsia shawl was draped over her right shoulder.

Why does she always dress like a color-blind gypsy? Liz wondered. *With all her money, Dr. M-C should be able to pull together an outfit that doesn't make her look as if she's a refugee from a circus.*

"Elizabeth!" said Dr. M-C, tucking another pencil in her hair. "Just the person I was looking for!"

"Hey there, Dr. Markham-Collins, I was . . ."

"Yes, yes, fine," Dr. M-C said, talking over Liz. "Can you tell me where Heather is? I need to speak with her."

Probably hiding somewhere, Liz thought. She shrugged. "I don't know."

"'Don't know?'" Dr. M-C repeated. She peered at Liz over her glasses. "What do you mean, you don't know where my daughter is. What do I pay you for?"

"She was here a minute ago," Liz explained, "and I was just going to go—"

"Heather!" Dr. M-C shouted, making Liz wince. Dr. M-C tended to bellow. Liz was surprised the windows didn't shatter on a regular basis.

Heather appeared in the doorway, trailed closely by

David. David was sturdy little kid with dark brown hair and big brown eyes. As far as Liz could tell, he was the most normal person in the household.

"Heather, there you are, darling," Dr. M-C boomed. "I have WONDERFUL news for you."

"What, Mommy?" Heather asked nervously. She glanced at Liz with fearful eyes. Both Liz and Heather knew that Dr. M-C's so-called brilliant ideas were usually anything but.

"I was speaking with Mitzi Huntington this morning," Dr. M-C gushed, "and Mitzi said that Kelli is just *thriving* these days, and she has riding lessons to thank for it. She says that Kelli has just *blossomed* thanks to all the fresh air and exercise."

She bent down to look Heather in the eye. The little girl shrank into the corner. "I worry about you, darling. You're so pasty and nervous all the time. What you need is a good dose of the outdoors, some healthy competition, and some solid discipline. Riding, it is!"

"Riding what?" Heather asked.

"Why, HORSES, darling!" Dr. M-C stood back up and clapped her hands lightly. "Gorgeous, talented, horse-show horses!"

"Do the horses sing and dance in the show?" David asked.

"No, silly!" Liz said, grabbing David and tickling him.

"Come on. You know better than that!"

"Of course, he does," Dr. M–C said testily. "David is an exceptionally bright boy." She turned back to Heather. "In horse shows, the rider leaps over fences, jumps over hedges, races across muddy turf—all to show the skills of the horse and the rider."

"I–I don't like horses," Heather protested weakly. "They're big, and they smell."

"Nonsense!" said Dr. M–C. "You'll love it." Now she addressed Liz. "This is the PERFECT activity for Heather to be involved in. The Devlins own a horse farm out in the country, now don't they?"

"I don't know," Liz admitted. Liz knew that Dr. M–C, as well as every girl in the New York City private school set, was still reeling from shock that Parker was into *her*. Actually, at times Liz couldn't believe it herself. But she would never give her boss the satisfaction of admitting that she often had no idea how her own boyfriend felt about her.

"Well, of course I know they do," Dr. M–C said. "The Knickerbocker Junior Equestrian Competition is coming up. There is just enough time for Heather to learn to ride, get good at it, and win a silver cup at the Knickerbocker to reinforce the positive nature of her new activity."

This is such *a bad idea,* Liz thought. *A horse show? With a kid who has never been on a horse?*

Liz knew the real reason Dr. M–C was pushing Heather

into riding was the prestige of being part of the horse show and the horsey set. If Mitzi Huntington's daughter rode horses, well, then Dr. M-C's daughter would, too!

Dr. M-C picked up the phone and began dialing. "You'll see, Heather, you will simply adore it." Dr. M-C spoke into the phone as Heather slunk over to Liz and gripped her hand. "Claremont Riding Academy? This is Dr. Mayra Markham-Collins calling . . . why yes, it *is* the same Dr. Markham-Collins who wrote the bestselling child psychology book *Good Boy, Bad Boy, My Boy, Your Boy*. How kind of you to say so." Dr. M-C beamed. Liz rolled her eyes. Dr. M-C loved being famous.

"Yes," Dr. M-C continued, "I would like to set up lessons for my daughter, Miss Heather Markham-Collins. No, not at all, she ADORES horses. . . ."

"Mommy, I don't!" Heather dashed forward and tugged her mother's arm.

"Well, nooooo, not an expert. She has had *some* experience, but really she needs work on everything."

Liz shook her head. The only experience Heather had with horses were the wooden ones on the Central Park carousel. And even *those* scared the little girl.

Dr. M-C shook Heather's arm off and kept talking. "Good. We'll see you Monday afternoon. Where do you suggest we go to get her supplies?"

"But, *Mommy!*" Heather shrieked.

Dr. M-C glared at Heather with a look that instantly silenced her. Heather knew when she was beaten.

"Copperfields it is, then," Dr. Collins said. She hung up, a broad grin on her wide face. "Liz," she said, "tomorrow I want you to take Heather to Copperfields. You are to ask for Eleanor. She will organize everything that Heather needs."

"Yes, Dr. Markham-Collins." Like Heather, Liz knew when it was useless to argue.

"Good! That's all settled!" Dr. Markham-Collins swept out of the room. The kitchen instantly seemed larger.

"Please, Liz, don't make me!" Heather begged.

"Don't worry, Heather," Liz said soothingly. "It will be fine! You'll love it!"

And I'm a big fat liar!

CHAPTER THREE

the deals

Adrienne cringed at the sound of a loud and crashing chord.

"I hate Mendelssohn," Emma whined. She slammed the piano keyboard shut. "He doesn't know one iota about composition!"

Adrienne hid a smile. Emma was so far advanced for her age that it was nice to see her throw a normal kid-fit for a change. "I don't know, Emma," she teased. "He *has* kind of survived the test of time."

Emma glared at Adrienne. "Ohhhhhhhh-kay," she moaned. She started practicing again.

Adrienne settled more comfortably on the sofa and stared down at her homework. Luckily, her cell phone rang. Adrienne glanced at the screen: Lily Singh.

"Hey, there, Adrienne!" Lily greeted her in her ever-cheerful voice. She was one of Adrienne's closest friends at Van Rensselaer High, the best public school in the city, where they were both juniors.

"Hey, Lily, what's up?"

"Tamara and I are going to Café Dante in the Village," Lily said. "Why don't you come, too? We might catch a movie since it's Friday. Avoid homework till tomorrow."

"Sounds cool!" Adrienne said, glancing at her watch. "It's already dinnertime. I just have to wait for Mrs. Warner to come home so I can get paid."

"Excellent. Invite Liz, too," Lily said. "See you later!" She clicked off.

Adrienne was just about to dial Liz when she heard the elevator door opening into the vestibule of the Warners' apartment. Adrienne crossed into the entrance hall, hoping that it would be Mrs. Warner.

A small dog with tufts of hair raced into the hall and promptly hid under a credenza. The dog was followed by four doormen carrying bags from Alexander McQueen, Stella McCartney, Prada, and Dior.

Oh, no, Adrienne thought, her shoulders sagging. *It's Cameron!*

Even though Adrienne was over Brian, she would never forget the way Cameron had treated her. She had befriended Adrienne solely to steal her boyfriend. She used Adrienne to throw parties just so there would be someone to blame in case they got caught. And every chance Cameron got, she found a way to put Adrienne down.

"Thanks, guys," Cameron said to the porters. She handed each of them a crisp $100 bill as they stepped back into the elevator.

"What a day!" Cameron said, smoothing the front of her Roberto Cavalli top. "I am totally shopped out."

"Sorry it was so rough, Cam," Adrienne said. "Listen, do you know when your stepmom is coming home? I'm only scheduled till Emma's dinnertime, and she owes me five hundred dollars for last week."

"Oh, *wow*," Cameron said, her nearly silver eyes wide. "Is that why Christine gave me five hundred dollars this morning? I just used it for tips for the boys downstairs." She laughed. "I mean, how could I know that you *only* make five hundred dollars. I was afraid that I wasn't tipping enough!"

Adrienne's jaw tensed. *Fine,* she thought. *You want to be that way?* She could play Cameron's put-down game, too. After all, she'd learned from the best: Cameron herself.

"Cam, when you were out shopping, did you go from Bergdorf's to Alexander McQueen down in the meatpacking district?" Adrienne asked.

"Sure," Cameron replied, tossing her long, white-blond hair over one shoulder. "Why?"

"Oh, I was just wondering if you had seen the huge banner hanging across the front of the New York Public Library," Adrienne said. "You know the one. It has an enormous picture of Mimi von Fallschirm on it."

Cameron winced as if she had been hit. *Score!* Adrienne thought triumphantly. Mimi was a sore topic for Cameron, and Adrienne knew it.

"I did," Cameron said, glowering. "I can't believe that her big-nosed, fat old face is up there. It should have been ME on that poster."

"But you didn't win Deb of the Year," Adrienne reminded Cameron sweetly—just in case Cam had recently had a lobotomy and didn't remember the crushing defeat. For the girls in Cameron's orbit, being named Debutante of the Year was the be-all and end-all of making it in "society."

"And," Adrienne added, "Mimi is a *princess*, Cam. You can't top that. You'll just have to face the fact that she's the committee chair for the Young Lions of the New York Public Library. Just one of the perks of being Deb of the Year."

"It's so unfair!" Cameron moaned. "I should be the committee chair." Her eyes narrowed. "And trust me, I will be."

"Isn't it a little late?" Adrienne smirked.

"It is never too late. Not for me. I was meant to be the chair, and I will be." Cameron gave Adrienne a sweet smile. "And *you're* going to help me."

"No way, Cameron," Adrienne said.

"If you don't help me," Cameron said, "I would

wonder how much longer you'll be working here." She did a flawless imitation of her stepmother: "Adriana, we are a *family*, and *families* help one another."

Adrienne sighed. She'd heard that refrain all too many times.

"Besides," Cameron added, the sweet routine dropped entirely. "We had a deal, remember?"

"What deal?" Adrienne asked innocently, but she cringed inside. She had hoped Cameron had forgotten their conversation at the Manhattan Cotillion. To her great relief, Cameron hadn't brought it up again in the two weeks that had passed.

Cameron pointed her perfectly manicured finger at Adrienne. "Now don't pretend you don't remember, darling. You know perfectly well what I'm talking about." Cameron took a step closer. Instinctively, Adrienne shrank back as if Cameron were contagious.

"You help me dethrone Princess Mimi von *Foul*-schirm," Cameron crooned, draping her thin, silk-clad arm across Adrienne's shoulder, "and I will let you in on the secret Parker Devlin is keeping from your gal-pal Liz. And, believe me, this is something she really must know."

Adrienne sighed. There was definitely some kind of trouble between Liz and Parker. Their relationship alternated between awesome and awful.

"So. . . ?" Cameron wheedled. "Will you hold up your

part of the bargain?"

Adrienne sighed again. Cameron could make her life hell, as she had in the past. Besides, what did she care if Mimi was toppled from her position as a chair of some benefit Adrienne would never attend?

"Fine. I'll help you," Adrienne said. "So what is this big secret of Parker's?"

"No, no, no." Cameron smiled her megawatt smile. "First you help me. *Then* I help you."

Adrienne was getting frustrated. She had experienced this trapped feeling far too frequently since becoming a nanny. If it wasn't Mrs. Warner somehow getting her to put in extra time with extra responsibilities, it was Cameron stringing her along, just as she was doing right now.

"What exactly do you want me to do?" Adrienne asked. She braced herself for the worst, since the worst was generally what Cameron had to offer.

Cameron put a finger to her porcelain cheek as if she were thinking hard. "Well, that's just it. I haven't come up with the perfect plan—yet. But when I do, you'll be the first to know!" Cameron turned to leave, and then stopped.

"Oh, and Adrienne," Cameron added, smiling, "I was so teasing you about the money. Christine still has it. Ciao!"

Adrienne shut her eyes and counted to ten. Twice. She only opened them after she could no longer hear Cameron's Manolos clicking on the marble floor.

"Adriana?" a familiar voice called from the hallway lead-ing to the bedrooms. "Is that you?" It was Christine Olivia Warner, Cameron's stepmom and Adrienne's employer.

She's been home all along? Adrienne thought. *I wish I had known—I'd have been so out of here.*

"Yes, Mrs. Warner?" Adrienne called back. Adrienne had learned to answer to almost any name since in all this time the COW rarely managed to get her name right.

Mrs. Warner appeared at the door of her suite. She was dressed in elegant, bone-colored silk trousers and a pale peach blouse that flattered her cosmetically enhanced skin. Her blond hair was well-sprayed. "There you are!" she said. "At last. I need your help on a number of things. . . ."

"Um, Mrs. Warner?" Adrienne said, noticing once again that the COW always managed to come up with her *correct* name when she was asking for a favor. "My day is actually over, and I need to get going."

Adrienne spoke very quickly so that Mrs. Warner couldn't interrupt her. The COW had an infuriating ability to rope Adrienne into all kinds of extra tasks. Adrienne was determined to finally set some boundaries with this wacky family.

Mrs. Warner raised an eyebrow as far as her Botox would let her.

"In fact," Adrienne continued, "I was just waiting around until you could pay me. . . ?"

"Oh, very well," Mrs. Warner said, clearly irritated. She vanished for a moment, then returned holding out several crisp bills. "Here." She handed Adrienne the money.

"Thanks!" Adrienne said good-bye to Emma and picked up her backpack in the hall closet. She raced to the kitchen to hop into the service elevator—and freedom.

"Hey! What's your hurry, gorgeous?" Adrienne stopped. It was Graydon Warner, Cameron's older half brother. His silky brown hair, dark eyes, square jaw, and killer bod did nothing to disguise the fact that he was a total sleaze. He was always trying to cop a feel, or was making lewd remarks, and was generally annoying to Adrienne. This was the first time she'd seen him since the Manhattan Cotillion, and she really hoped it would be her last for a loooooong while.

"Gotta go, Graydon," Adrienne said. "See you around."

"Of course you will," Graydon said. "After all, we have a hot date."

"Yeah, sure," Adrienne said. "Dream on."

"Why so mean?" Graydon pouted. Then he ginned a sly, slow grin. "You remember our deal, don't you?"

Adrienne blinked. She had totally forgotten. *I must have blocked it because it was just too horrible to remember,* Adrienne thought. *First Cameron and now this?*

"You said that if I helped you and Liz get into the Manhattan Cotillion, you would go on one date with me,"

Graydon said. "So when do I collect?"

Adrienne sighed. It was true. Liz had begged Adrienne to agree to Graydon's demands. Parker was *that* important to Liz, and Liz was that important to Adrienne. Without Graydon's help, they never would have gotten into the ball. Liz would never have gotten Parker back that night, Adrienne would never have realized what a loser her ex-boyfriend Brian was, and Adrienne wouldn't have seen Cam's humiliated face when she lost Deb of the Year to Princess Mimi von Fallschirm. Watching Cameron lose almost made the promise worthwhile.

Almost.

"Don't nannies keep their promises?" Graydon pressed.

Adrienne shuddered. "All right," she said. "One date and that is it. *One!* No groping, no gross behavior, you pay, and I can go home whenever I want. Deal?"

Graydon laughed. "You drive a hard bargain, Adrienne. I like that. Let's make it tomorrow night— before you can figure out a way to back out. Seven thirty. You work Saturday, right? I'll pick you up here."

"Whatever, Graydon." Adrienne stepped into the waiting elevator and pushed the button.

"See you then." Graydon winked at her as the elevator door closed.

"Ugh," Adrienne groaned. *How did my best friend's love life make* my *life so complicated?*

CHAPTER FOUR

gotta take this

On Saturday Liz made sure to get home from outfitting Heather at Copperfields with plenty of time to get ready for her date with Parker. They were going to Jack Chasen's party, and Liz dressed with special care. The deep burgundy silk Ghost dress—paid for by saving several weeks of nanny pay—made her pale skin shimmer and emphasized her long legs. She pulled her dark curls into a ponytail, letting soft tendrils frame her face. The look was sexy—and casual chic. Just what she wanted. She hadn't spent a lot of time with Parker's superrich friends, and she wanted to make sure she made a good impression—or, at least, fit in.

There were still times when insecurity overcame Liz, and Parker's occasional erratic behavior cast a gloom over her sunny worldview. It didn't help that Liz had met Parker through Cameron Warner. Cameron and her satellites seemed to take delight in making Liz feel as if she were a scholarship wannabe among the legitimate privileged class.

They were all stunned when it turned out that Parker wasn't just slumming with Liz—that he actually seemed to genuinely care for her.

"Have I mentioned yet that you are the hottest girl here?" Parker asked as they walked into Jack Chasen's townhouse on East Seventieth Street.

"Twice," Liz said, smiling up at him. "I might just start to believe it—"

"You should," Jack interrupted, "'cause it's true. Devlin, take your date's coat so I can get her a drink and try to steal her away from you."

Liz giggled, enjoying the attention, and glad to know that Jack *was* really joking; he had been dating Miranda Dalziel for months, and everyone knew it.

Parker helped Liz off with her coat and disappeared in search of the attendant hired for the evening.

"Come on," Jack said. "Let me get you something to drink."

Liz followed Jack into the dining room. It was large and basically empty, except for the huge mahogany table covered with wine, beer, and fixings for mixed drinks. Scattered around the room were kids from Parker's world: the superrich set. Liz nodded at a few faces she recognized from Pheasant-Berkeley School for Girls or from other dates with Parker.

"What's your pleasure?" Jack asked, picking up an

empty crystal glass from the enormous table.

"Me, I hope," Parker said, stepping up behind Liz. He put his hand on the small of her back, sending delicious shivers up her spine.

"You'll do for now," Liz teased.

Parker grinned. "I think I can take over from here, Jack."

"Enjoy," Jack said, putting the glass back down. He wandered off to greet a couple who had just arrived.

"I'm glad Jack didn't manage to steal you away from me," Parker said, wrapping his hands around Liz's waist.

"Not possible," Liz said, stretching up to give him a kiss.

"Good," Parker said, reaching into his pocket and pulling out a small box. "Then I don't have to return this."

Liz recognized the orange box of the House of Hermès. Smiling at Parker, she opened it.

A heavy gold bracelet lay inside, made of the chains and links of horse bridles.

"I thought you could use it since you're going to be hanging out at the stables," Parker said, grinning.

Liz was touched by the thoughtful gift—and blown away by the incredible quality, not to mention the *cost* of the beautiful bracelet. "I can't believe that you remembered that I have to start taking Heather to riding lessons next week."

"I always try to know where you are," Parker said. "Gotta keep an eye on you!"

He leaned in to give her a real kiss, but before his lips touched Liz's, his cell phone rang.

Parker straightened up and pulled out his cell. He glanced down at the number on the phone display.

"Gotta take this," he said. "I'll be right back." Without waiting for Liz to respond, he spun around and left the room.

I hate *that cell phone!* Liz thought. Irritated, she stalked over to the table and picked up some grapes. She popped one into her mouth and looked around the room. The party seemed to be couples only, and everyone was moving quickly into make-out mode.

And here I am, alone and stuffing my face, Liz thought. *That is so typical.* Liz dropped the grapes back on the table and went downstairs to find Parker.

Liz peeked into a library and a music room, and finally into the kitchen, where she startled two large Persian cats that immediately leaped onto counters and hissed at her. "Thanks," Liz said sarcastically to the cats. "Like I don't already feel like I'm trespassing."

Liz looked out the kitchen window into the garden and saw Parker standing alone, talking into his cell phone. *He looks serious,* Liz thought. Concerned, she quickly slipped outside.

". . . so what does this mean for us, then?" Parker said, his voice trembling.

Us? Liz screamed inside her head. She felt her heart begin to thud hard.

Parker turned and noticed her standing there. "I have to go," he said into the phone in a flat voice. "I'll talk to you later." He snapped the phone shut and looked at Liz with hollow eyes.

"Parker," Liz said, "who were you talking to?"

"No one. Let's not talk about it," he said. He took her arm and steered her back inside. He made a beeline for the drinks table and grabbed a beer. Downing it quickly, he scanned the room. "Music sucks."

"Parker, what is going on?" Liz asked, hating how whiny her voice sounded.

Parker didn't even look at her. He just picked up another beer. "It's a total nothing, Liz."

"But—"

"Drop it," Parker snapped.

Liz stared at him, shocked by his tone.

He poured a glass of champagne and handed it to Liz. "I believe this is what you were drinking," he said, sounding normal again. Actually, Liz realized, he sounded as if he was trying really hard to sound normal again. Like it was an effort.

"Thanks," she said, taking the glass. She noticed the new bracelet dangling on her wrist. A moment ago she had been delirious at Parker's considerate gesture and extraordinary gift. Now, she didn't know what to feel. One minute she had been on top of the world with Parker, and then something happened to plummet her right into misery.

And worse—she was starting to get used to it.

"Wasn't that the best party?" Emma said. It was early Saturday evening, and the goody bag the little girl was lugging off the elevator was so overloaded, Adrienne had to help her drag it into the Warners' apartment.

"Sadly, Emma," Adrienne said, "I totally agree with you." It was a pathetic day when a sixteen-year-old had to admit that the eight-year-old birthday party she attended was more fabulous than her wedding would probably be. *And definitely more fun than my date with Graydon will be tonight.*

"Normally I find birthday parties juvenile," Emma said, hoisting the bag onto her bed. "But this one surpassed my expectations."

"I know you aren't crazy about Jessica Carmichael, but her family is important to your parents," Adrienne said. "Aren't you glad your mother made you go?" She hoped Emma would start being more open to play dates. It would make being her nanny a lot easier. Now Adrienne was all the company Emma had—and it meant Adrienne had to really stay on her toes.

Emma ignored the question and pulled a three-pound

box of Jacques Torres chocolates from the bag. Next she held up a CD of the band that had played at the party.

"That band was great," Adrienne said. "How did the Carmichaels manage to get them to play for a pack of eight-year-olds?"

"I think her dad owns the band," Emma said. "Or the studio that produced the band. Or the country the band is from. Something."

"Ah," Adrienne said with a nod. Made sense in Warner-land. "You unload the rest of your loot while I run your bath. It's almost bedtime."

Adrienne walked into Emma's bathroom and turned the gold-plated taps shaped like swan's heads. As the tub filled, she poured in the Annick Goutal Eau d'Hadrien bubble bath the little girl liked. At thirty-eight dollars for a miniscule bottle, it was a far cry from the Mr. Bubble Adrienne had used at Emma's age.

Water filled the marble tub, the heat making Adrienne's skin feel moist.

I'd better be careful, she thought. *If I don't get out of here, my hair will frizz up and I'll look goofy for this stupid date with Graydon.*

Adrienne caught sight of herself in the mirror and a slow smile spread across her face. She turned on the hot water in the sink, letting it run.

Emma opened the door to the clouds of billowing

steam. "Are you trying to cook me?" she squeaked.

"Come in!" Adrienne said, giggling. "Quick, close the door!"

"What are you doing?" Emma asked.

"I'm helping you with your bath."

"I don't need help with my bath," Emma said indignantly. "Besides I don't consider *boiling* me helping." She bit her lip and narrowed her eyes. "I should write this down."

"Write what down?" Adrienne asked.

"Your erratic behavior," Emma explained. "You generally exhibit *basically* normal teenage behavior. But now and then you manifest tendencies of mania that indicate possible mental disturbance." Emma dashed out of the bathroom.

Adrienne looked in the mirror with satisfaction as her hair slowly rose into its natural state of unruly frizz and her skin grew pink and blotchy from the heat.

Emma reentered carrying her leather-bound notebook and a Cartier pencil. She studied Adrienne for a moment, then began to scribble furiously. "Could you turn the steam down?" she demanded. "My pages are shriveling up!"

Emma wrote a few more sentences, then placed the notebook in the corner farthest away from the steaming tub. She took off her robe and carefully tested the water with one toe. "At least it's not boiling," she said as she slipped into the bubbles.

"Is it all right?" Adrienne asked. Maybe she *had* gone a little heavy on the hot water. The mirror was now completely fogged over.

"It's nice," Emma said, splashing bubbles at Adrienne.

I wonder where Graydon is taking me? Adrienne thought as she leaned into the steam rising from the sink. *If I play my cards right, I'll be home and in bed before* "Weekend Update" *on* Saturday Night Live. *And this whole stupid date thing will be over with forever.*

"I'm getting pruney," Emma announced. "Time to get out."

"So soon?" Adrienne asked.

"Adrienne," Emma whined.

"Okay, okay." Adrienne turned off the tap in the sink and helped the little girl climb out of the oversized tub. Adrienne made sure to splash herself with the bathwater.

Emma clutched her now slightly damp notebook to her chest as she got into bed.

"Don't stay up too late writing," Adrienne said, turning on the bedside lamp.

"I won't," Emma promised. "I just have to get down how weird you are." She tapped her pencil on her notebook. "I need to keep closer tabs on you in case you go psycho."

"Sweet dreams to you, too, Emma," Adrienne said, smiling. While Emma wrote in her notebook, Adrienne shut off the overhead light and left the room.

Cameron passed her in the hallway. "Your date has arrived," she said. Her eyes traveled up and down Adrienne. "And I'd say he's in for quite a surprise."

"Oh, I think we girls should keep boys guessing, don't you?" Adrienne said.

"I just hope Graydon is taking you someplace dark. Because looking like that, there is no lighting that can flatter." Cameron turned and strolled down the hallway to her room as if it were a runway lined with photographers.

Adrienne walked out to the Warners' enormous entry hall. The setting sun glowed through the skylight and was reflected in the mirrored walls and chandeliers, bathing Graydon in soft pink light. *Maybe once he gets a look at me, he'll run screaming into the night,* Adrienne thought. *Oh, please please please.*

"Here I am!" Adrienne announced. Graydon turned, and Adrienne grinned up at him, her hair frizzed into a reddish Afro, her ultracasual, long jersey skirt clinging to her legs, her oversized cotton shirt lank and loose. Her skin was blotchy and damp, and her hands were red and chafed from the hot water of Emma's bath.

Graydon grabbed her hand, pulling her to him. "Mmmm," he murmured. "Eau d'Hadrien. Very sophisticated." He smiled. "Or is that Eau D'Adrienne?"

Oh, puh-lease, Adrienne thought, stepping away from

him. "Okay, Graydon," she said. "Let's get this date over with."

Now Graydon looked surprised. "Don't you want to go change?"

"You don't like my outfit?" Adrienne said. "I'm so hurt."

"But—" Graydon stopped himself and shrugged. "You're the boss. Let's go."

When they stepped outside, Graydon nodded to the Rolls-Royce waiting at the curb, chauffeur at the ready. "The car's right here."

Adrienne got into the fancy car, reluctantly admiring its highly polished wood interior and inhaling the scent of the soft leather.

"So," Graydon said, slipping in beside her. "Are you ready to take a trip to another world?" He pulled a bottle of Veuve Clicquot from an ice bucket and poured two glasses of champagne.

Adrienne snorted. "Yeah, right. I'm not going anywhere 'otherworldly' with you."

"How about Moscow?" Graydon asked, handing her the crystal flute of champagne. "It's definitely different."

Startled, Adrienne spilled champagne on the leather seat. *He has* got *to be kidding me.* She stared at him, her green eyes wide with horror. "You're not serious?" she demanded. "Moscow? As in Russia?"

"Not exactly," Graydon said. "But close."

"I-I don't have a passport," Adrienne blurted.

Graydon smiled at her over his champagne flute. "You don't need one."

The Warners' private jet, Adrienne remembered. *Of course.*

She shut her eyes, forcing down her panic. *This would be totally like him,* she realized. The over-the-top grand gesture. Whisking her off without a thought about how she would feel, and worse—putting her in a situation where she would be trapped alone with him. In a foreign country!

The idea of being helpless and dependent on Graydon destroyed all her efforts to stay calm.

Instinctively, Adrienne reached for the door handle. All she could think of was escape—even if it meant jumping out of a moving car in the middle of traffic.

Graydon laughed and grabbed her hand. "We may be only inching down Fifth Avenue, but I'm still not going to let you hurl yourself out into the street."

"I am *not* leaving the city with you," Adrienne said firmly. "Much less the country."

"You're really something, Adrienne," Graydon said. "A lot of girls would be thrilled to go out with me." He shook his head. "Fine, so you're not, and I know it. I forced you into this, but you might at least try to have a good time. You'll never have to do it again. Besides, you might actually have fun. I'm not such an ogre."

"Jury's still out on that," Adrienne muttered.

Graydon slid farther away from her on the seat. He held up his hands in an "I surrender" gesture. "I'm cool, Queen of all Nannies. Just relax, okay?"

"Ooooh-kay," Adrienne said cautiously. "So, where are we going?"

"I told you," Graydon said, his devilish smile returning. "Moscow!"

CHAPTER FIVE

Moscow on the Hudson

Adrienne kept her eyes on the streets outside, trying to figure out where on earth Graydon was taking her.

What is he up to? she wondered as they rode over a bridge from Manhattan into Brooklyn. Adrienne's stomach churned as she watched the streets grow dark and deserted. She peered out the windows, trying to get her bearings. She moved as far from Graydon as she could, fear making her throat tight. *Will the chauffeur help me if Graydon tries something awful?*

The signs on the stores indicated they were now in Brighton Beach, a neighborhood far out in Brooklyn—nearly to the ocean. As the Rolls slowed, Adrienne didn't see any beach—all she saw was enormous, deserted-looking warehouses.

I've watched enough CSI *with Emma to know that this totally looks like the scene of a crime,* Adrienne thought.

"That's it," Adrienne said firmly. "I've had enough!

Where are we? What are we doing out here?"

"You'll see," Graydon said.

Graydon's little mysterious act seriously pissed her off. "Tell me or I won't get out," Adrienne threatened.

"Fine!" Graydon threw up his hands. "This is only the hottest, coolest, little-known famous club in Brighton Beach!" He rolled his eyes. "I *wanted* to surprise you."

The car drove around one of the dark warehouses and parked. Adrienne now saw that the building up ahead wasn't empty. In fact, there was a crowd at the entrance.

"You should have told me," Adrienne said.

"What did you think I was planning?" Graydon asked. He looked at her expression and added, "On second thought—don't answer that."

They walked up to the brightly lit entrance. Dozens of well-dressed couples stood outside, waiting to be allowed in. The women were model-thin, and all seemed to be draped in Versace or Dolce & Gabbana, the men in hip suits.

The bouncer spotted Graydon and immediately lifted the velvet rope. "Meester Varner!" he greeted in a heavy Russian accent. "Good eeevininng!"

That's right, Adrienne thought, remembering what she knew about Brighton Beach. *There's a big Russian immigrant population out here.*

"*Dobrei vecher!*" Gradyon replied, shaking his hand.

Graydon speaks Russian? Adrienne stared at him.

When they entered the huge space, Adrienne gawked at the surroundings. The place was an old movie palace, and the gilded balcony still stretched around the room. The former orchestra area was now a huge dance floor surrounded by tables and chairs, and the band and DJ were up on the old stage. The room was packed: rich-looking Russians with their model-type girlfriends were doing shots at the bar or dancing, or nibbling appetizers. A smattering of older couples sat at tables looking like regulars enjoying the Russian atmosphere. The tables were covered with so many bottles of vodka and champagne and sumptuous hors d'oeuvres that Adrienne was surprised they didn't collapse.

"I told you we were going to Moscow!" Graydon shouted over the loud music. "It's something, huh?"

It sure is, Adrienne thought. She caught sight of herself in a mirror. *And so am I!* She frantically tried to calm her hair, raking through it with her fingers. *I wanted to embarrass Graydon, but it looks like the only person who is embarrassed is me!*

"Uh, Graydon?" Adrienne said as they reached their table. "I'm going to run to the ladies' room to . . . uh . . ."

"Freshen up?" Graydon asked. His trademark smirk returned, but this time it didn't make Adrienne mad. She deserved it.

Keeping her backpack with her, Adrienne made her

way to the lavish gold-and-crystal-filled restroom. The other women inside stared at her.

"*Uzhastnaya,*" said one woman to another, giggling.

"What did you say?" Adrienne asked, knowing that she was not getting a compliment.

"Dreadful," replied the women's friend. "Such a nice restaurant, and you come looking like . . ."

"I know, I know," Adrienne said. She studied herself in the mirror. *Time for the extreme makeover.*

Adrienne opened her backpack. She pulled out makeup, hair gel, and a brush. The first thing she needed to do was tame her unruly frizz. She stuck her head in the sink, wet her hair, then slicked it back, pulling it into a sleek ponytail.

Adrienne evened out her blotchy skin tone with light foundation, then gave herself dramatic eyes in khaki and gold, which brought out the red of her hair and green of her eyes. Natural lip liner and gloss completed the simple look. Adrienne could see the women around her beginning to nod in approval.

Adrienne squinted at her reflection. *Now the outfit.*

The oversized white shirt she'd borrowed from her father's closet was completely shapeless, and her skirt was not a flattering length. What to do?

Suddenly, Adrienne had an idea. She grabbed the stretchy waistband and pulled the jersey skirt up so the hem hit above her knees. Then she folded over the top of the skirt to make a wide, flat waistband that lay low on her hips. *That works,* she decided.

She couldn't just take off the man-tailored shirt, because the tank she was wearing underneath it had birthday cake stains on it. *I know!* She unbuttoned the shirt and took the two front corners, wrapped them once around her waist, then tied them on one side. In a final touch, she flicked up the collar. The new style emphasized her small waist and looked as if she had actually put the outfit together on purpose.

"*Krasivaya!*" exclaimed the women standing at the mirrors. "Beautiful!"

"Thank you!" she said. She picked up a perfume off the counter and gave herself a quick spritz. *At least now I don't have to be embarrassed!*

Adrienne walked back to the table and, with great pleasure, noticed that many of the men were staring at her appreciatively. And the women weren't shooting her dirty looks anymore.

"Wow," Graydon said, standing and pulling her chair out for her. "You keep a new outfit in that bag?"

"Just tricks," Adrienne replied.

"You're full of surprises, aren't you?" Graydon said as he sat back down.

"Just keeping you on your toes," Adrienne quipped.

By the time they'd finished their entrees, Adrienne had come to the astounding realization that Graydon wasn't so bad after all.

He was studying international business, had spent his summer sessions in Moscow, and had learned Russian while he was there. Clearly he wasn't the slacker dope Adrienne had assumed he was. He liked the same bands she did, including a few almost no one else had ever heard of; he agreed Cameron was the pits; and he even loved to go to the same funky dive hamburger place near Columbia University that she did.

She studied him over her dessert. *Could I have been wrong about him?*

"Want to dance?" Graydon asked, as the band struck up a slow Russian song.

Adrienne cocked her head. "Why not?" she said.

They got to the middle of the dance floor, and Graydon took Adrienne in his arms. She braced herself for his usual groping, but his hands stayed exactly where they should.

Wow, Adrienne thought as they slowly moved around the dance floor. *This guy knows what he's doing.* Her ex-boyfriend Brian hated dancing—the best he would do was rock from side to side when his favorite metal bands played. But Graydon had the confident moves of a Fred

Astaire or a Gene Kelly from the old black-and-white movie musicals her grandparents tried to force her to watch.

Adrienne listened to the strange language, and the soft beautiful sounds swirled in her head.

"What is he singing?" Adrienne asked, looking up at Graydon.

Graydon concentrated, listening to the music for a second; then, lowering his head to her ear, he translated in a husky whisper:

> *"Who would have thought,*
> *I'd be so lucky?*
> *Who would have thought*
> *it would be you and I,*
> *here tonight?*
> *Who would have thought*
> *that a girl like you*
> *would be here*
> *with a guy like me?*
> *And you should know,*
> *You should think,*
> *I could love you. . . ."*

Adrienne gazed up at Graydon, intoxicated by the lovely words. He was smiling down at her with a serious expression, gazing deeply into her eyes.

He's going to kiss me! Adrienne realized. And, to her astonishment, the idea didn't completely nauseate her.

She leaned her head back, preparing to be kissed, when the music stopped. Graydon released her, and she ducked her head to cover her embarrassment. She applauded along with everyone else.

"I guess I should get you home, huh?" Graydon asked. "Unlike my oh-so-involved parents, yours are probably waiting up for you."

Adrienne noted the edge in his voice. Did he wish for a more normal family? One with limits and rules? She had always figured he was just like Cameron: uncontrollable and happy that way. If Adrienne behaved like Cameron and her friends, her parents would lock her up and have heart attacks. Not necessarily in that order.

"I guess you're right," Adrienne said. *Am I actually feeling disappointed? How weird is that?*

In the car, Adrienne once again prepared for Graydon to pounce on her, but he didn't. As he chatted about the club, and Moscow, and school, Adrienne's mind reeled.

What is going on? This is the guy who has tried to grope me every time I've run into him. And now he's being Mr. Gentleman? What is wrong with this picture?

Before long, the car pulled up to Adrienne's corner in Morningside Heights near Columbia University, where her parents were professors.

"Well, this is me," Adrienne said.

"Can't I walk you to the door?" Graydon asked.

"This is fine," Adrienne said. "Graydon, thanks for tonight. . . . I was, um . . . surprised at what a good time I had."

"Thanks, Adrienne." Graydon seemed genuinely touched by her words. He smiled broadly. "Then I declare this date a total and complete success!"

Adrienne laughed, then slipped out of the Rolls. She waved at Graydon as the car drove away, aware of the gaping stares of the pedestrians. Not too many of them had seen a Rolls in the neighborhood before!

As she waited for the elevator, she realized she was humming the Russian tune she and Graydon had danced to. She felt a little dreamy, as if this had been a regular date, and she was looking forward to the next one.

Oh, my God, she thought. *I actually* am!

CHAPTER SIX

totally suspicious behavior

"So," Adrienne announced, slamming the metal door of her locker at Van Rensselaer High Monday afternoon, "it really wasn't so bad. I actually had a good time on my date with Graydon." She turned and looked at Lily and Tamara. "How weird is that?"

Tamara stared at Adrienne, her large brown eyes wide with disbelief. "On a weirdness scale of one to ten, I'd say it ranks about two hundred," she said.

"I *know!*" Adrienne said. "And what's even weirder? I think I want to go out with him again."

Lily's mouth dropped open.

Tamara snorted. "A few months ago, Mr. Perfect was flashing you in the bushes in Palm Beach and slipping into hot tubs with anyone with a pulse. Sorry. I just don't believe that Graydon had a complete personality overhaul."

Adrienne knew Tamara was trying to be helpful. She also knew Tamara wouldn't quit bugging her until she agreed. "Okay," Adrienne said. "I hear you."

"Good!" Tamara grinned, the subject obviously dropped—at least for now. "So, what's up after school? Do you all want to go hang out in the Village?"

"I can't." Adrienne sighed. "I have to head up to the Warners'."

"We'll walk you to the subway," Lily said, putting her arm through Adrienne's.

The three girls stepped out the front doors of Van Rensselaer High into the bright and crisp February day.

"What's going on?" Tamara said. "Why is everyone standing around the curb?"

Adrienne stood on tiptoe and tried to see over the crowd. As they moved closer, she realized what all the fuss was about.

The Warners' Rolls stood at the edge of the street, gleaming and black, its chrome fittings highly polished. The uniformed driver stood near the car, keeping the high school kids from getting too close.

Adrienne blinked. *Why would Mrs. Warner send the car for me? Is there some kind of an emergency? Do I have to take Emma somewhere?* Adrienne scanned her mental planner, trying to remember if Emma had appointments or special classes, but came up blank.

"Miss Adrienne!" the chauffeur called, waving as he spotted her.

Lily and Tamara turned and stared at Adrienne. "*Miss* Adrienne?" Lily said.

Adrienne shrugged. "It's a rich thing."

The three friends walked to the curb, the other kids parting for them as if they were celebrities. It felt strange to have all those eyes on her. Still, she had to admit it gave her kind of a thrill to be so important—to be someone who had a car sent for her. Like she was special.

"Hey, Adrienne," a girl from her math class called, "can I have your autograph?"

"You going to a funeral?" a boy from English shouted.

"Yeah, yours, if you don't quit hollering in my ear," the boy next to him grumbled.

Adrienne winced. This wasn't exactly the kind of attention she wanted.

"Master Warner had me bring the car to take you to work," the chauffer said.

"Now that's my kind of commute." Lily sighed enviously.

Adrienne sighed, too, but for a different reason. On the one hand, it was really sweet of Graydon to send her a ride to work, especially after she'd complained during their date about spending half her life on the subway. But it was such an over-the-top display. Typical Warner mentality.

She glanced at Tamara and Lily, who were practically drooling. *Well, at least I can share the wealth.*

"Say." Adrienne stepped up to the chauffeur. "Would it be all right if we dropped off my friends at Washington Square first?"

"Of course," the chauffeur replied, opening the door. "Please get in."

The three girls climbed into the backseat of the luxurious car.

"Oh, man," Tamara said, stretching her arms across the top of the backseat. She stroked the soft leather upholstery. "I have got to get me one of these after I make my platinum record!"

Lily looked stunned. "This car is bigger than my bedroom," she said with awe.

Suddenly, the voice of the driver startled them. "Master Graydon asked me to play this for you," he said. The sounds of the Russian song Adrienne and Graydon had danced to at the nightclub came through the speakers.

Adrienne shut her eyes, remembering how it felt to have Graydon's arms around her while they danced. It wasn't the fancy car that made her smile; it was the fact that Graydon had gone to such trouble to track down the CD.

You'd better watch out, Adrienne thought, leaning against the soft leather seat. *If you're not careful, you just might fall for the Graydon Warner charm!*

Adrienne stepped into the Warners' kitchen, singing the one line of the Russian song she could remember.

Emma jumped up from behind a counter, holding a tiny digital recorder.

"Got you!" she shrieked. "You're a foreign agent!"

"A what?" Adrienne stared down at the little blond girl.

"All day with this spying!" Tania wailed, throwing up her hands. "Miss Emma creeping around on floors like bug, with the machines and the peeping at the secrets!"

"What's up, Emma?" Adrienne said, giving Tania a sympathetic look. In addition to her housekeeping chores, Tania took care of Emma when Adrienne wasn't there.

"I told you," Emma said. "I am gathering evidence, *and...*," she whispered loudly, "I'm convinced that Kane is behind it!"

"Behind what?" Adrienne asked, wondering what on earth Emma could be talking about. Kane was the Warners' butler, and there was nothing about him that would make anyone think for a second that he was "*up to*" anything. In fact, he was rarely seen unless the Warners were entertaining.

"*It*," Emma intoned mysteriously.

"That's specific," Adrienne teased. "What exactly are you accusing him of?"

Emma pouted. "I don't know yet. That's why I have to keep an eye on him!"

"I think you've been watching too much *CSI*." Adrienne grabbed the little girl by the hand and steered her out of the kitchen. "Time for homework."

"And stop with the sneaky and the watching!" Tania called after them. Adrienne heard the woman muttering in Russian as the kitchen door swung shut behind them.

"Okay, what assignment do you want to work on first?" Adrienne pushed open the bedroom door. She was prepared for an argument. She wasn't prepared for the sight in front of her.

Emma's room had been done within an inch of its life by a famous decorator about a year ago. Adrienne had long admired the painted furniture and expensive upholstery. But the room was more of a stage set for a movie about a precious little rich girl than a sanctuary or a place to play. With its pink *strié* silk hangings, Impressionist paintings, and shelves of valuable antique dolls that held no interest for Emma, it was a room designed for Mrs. Warner's fantasy of a perfect, feminine, girlie daughter. Not the daughter she actually had.

Now Adrienne stared at all the changes.

Emma had pulled the silk curtains from their rods and stuffed them away somewhere, and bright afternoon light flooded the room. The dolls were piled in a corner and instead the shelves groaned under the weight of complicated electronic equipment. Emma had covered her walls with diagrams of the apartment and maps of the neighborhood, and on a far wall were pictures of every member of the Warner household, including a grinning picture of Adrienne, hair frizzed and skin blotchy from the previous weekend.

"Emma!" Adrienne shrieked. "How did you get this picture of me?"

"Camera behind a two-way mirror in the entry hall," Emma replied proudly.

Adrienne crossed to the wall and examined the pictures. Tania was grimacing, wiping the mirror with a cloth. Graydon was yawning. Cameron looked smugly pleased. Mrs. Warner was pulling the skin next to her eyes taut as if she was contemplating yet another lift. Mr. Warner was in profile; he obviously was the only Warner who wasn't obsessed with his appearance.

"Look at Kane," Emma ordered.

Adrienne peered at the picture of Kane. He was walking past the mirror carrying a small brown paper sack. "I don't see anything suspicious about this," she told Emma.

"That's because you haven't seen the video." Emma pointed a remote at the plasma TV on the wall.

"The *video*?" Adrienne repeated. She whirled around to face Emma. "You have been secretly *taping* people?"

"That's the best way to gather evidence," Emma said, speaking as if Adrienne were a complete idiot.

"Emma, you—"

"Shhh!" Emma ordered. "Here it comes."

Adrienne glanced at the screen. The camera was hidden somewhere in the hallway leading to the guest suites. The video showed Kane walking down the hall, still carrying his brown paper sack. He paused, then glanced around. He opened the door to one of the many guest powder rooms and shut it behind him.

I really hope this ends here, Adrienne thought. The idea of Emma hooking up cameras in bathrooms was just too awful to contemplate.

Luckily, the camera stayed trained on the bathroom door.

"I'll fast-forward." Emma hit a button and cued the tape to Kane's reappearance approximately twenty minutes later, according to the time code on the bottom of the screen.

"You see?" Emma said. "He's up to something. No one stays in the bathroom that long. At least, no one else I've videotaped."

Even though it did look fishy, Adrienne wasn't going to let Emma know that. She glanced at the screen. Now it showed Mr. Warner stumbling into the bathroom. It was obvious to Adrienne that Mr. Warner had been drinking, which was nothing unusual. But she didn't want Emma to know.

"Emma," Adrienne said. "The video stops *now*." She grabbed the remote from the little girl's hands and clicked it off.

"But, Adrienne," Emma protested. "I have to tape or I'll never solve any mysteries! That's always the best evidence."

"It is totally uncool to tape people without their knowledge," Adrienne said firmly. "In fact, it's illegal."

Emma rolled her eyes. "There are security cameras all over this stupid building and no one's upset about that."

The kid was right. As it often happened, Adrienne had to work hard to stay ahead of Emma. "That's different," Adrienne said, relieved she remembered *something* from civics class. "Those cameras are set up in public places. Your camera isn't. In a public place everyone knows they don't have any privacy. That's not true in your *home*."

Emma's jaw jutted defiantly. "I have the right to do whatever I want in my own *home*," she said, mimicking Adrienne's emphasis.

"You will stop it *now*," Adrienne said, "or I tell your mom."

Emma snorted derisively.

"No." Adrienne narrowed her eyes and crossed her arms over her chest. "I think I'll tell your father."

Emma swallowed, and Adrienne knew she had won.

"*And* you will erase any video you've already taken," Adrienne ordered. "If anyone sees that tape, Kane could get into trouble for no reason. You'll make people get the wrong idea."

"The wrong idea about what?" Cameron asked, standing in the doorway. "I love gossip."

"Sure, since if you're not making it, you're spreading it," Adrienne muttered.

"What?" Cameron stepped into the room.

Adrienne looked up and plastered a fake smile on her face. "Oh, nothing."

Cameron gave her a withering look as if she knew Adrienne had insulted her, then she flicked her long blond hair over her shoulder. "I don't have time for all this childishness," she announced. "I have an important essay to write."

She spun around on her Jimmy Choos and clattered down the hall.

"Cameron is actually doing her homework?" Emma said incredulously. "That is *totally* suspicious behavior."

Adrienne patted Emma on the shoulder. "You know, kiddo, this time I agree with you. That is way strange."

Before she left that evening, Adrienne made sure that Emma had disassembled her video feeds. The kid was so technologically advanced that all Adrienne could do was take Emma at her word and hope all of the surveillance cameras were gone.

She stepped into the street and shivered. She shoved her hands deeper into the pockets of her parka.

"Need a lift?" said a familiar voice from the curb.

Adrienne turned and spotted Graydon parked in the driver's seat of a hot little red Porsche 911 convertible. He was leaning out the window because, on this late February evening, he sensibly had the top closed.

"No Rolls?" Adrienne teased. "Forget it. I'd rather take the subway."

Graydon clutched his chest as if he were wounded. "Please?" he begged. "Give a guy a break!"

She looked at the car and then glanced in the direction of her subway stop. It would be a chilly walk to the subway, and then even more blocks to cover once she got uptown. "Weeelll. . . ," Adrienne said, acting as if she were mulling it over. "It *is* kind of cold out."

"Excellent!" Graydon leaned over to the passenger side and opened the door. "It's on my way, anyway. I'm heading up to Columbia."

"What are you doing here?" Adrienne asked once she settled in beside him. "I didn't see you upstairs."

Graydon gave her a slow smile. "Well, let's just say that after getting you *to* work in style this afternoon, I figured you deserved to go *home* in style, too."

"But how did you know when I'd leave?" Adrienne asked as the car headed west. She was torn again between thinking Graydon was being incredibly thoughtful and being really pushy. "Were you just sitting there waiting for me to come out?"

He tapped his forehead. "I have your schedule all up here."

Adrienne blinked. *Is he saying that he's been spying on me? Okay, that's just freaky.*

When the car pulled up in front of her building, Adrienne hopped out, slamming the door behind her.

"Thanks for the lift, Graydon," Adrienne said. She turned and dashed toward her building. She heard Graydon running to catch up with her.

"Hey, Adrienne!" Graydon said, stopping her and turning her around. "What's the problem?"

"The problem is I don't like stalkers," Adrienne told him. "It's really creepy to think some guy is checking up on you, learning your schedule, and then waiting around for you."

Graydon winced. "Wow," he said, "you really think I'm a scumbag." He sighed. "I guess I deserved that. But it's not the way you make it sound."

"Yeah? I think I described the situation pretty accurately."

Graydon ran his hand through his dark brown hair as

if massaging his head would help him think. "We don't go to the same school," he explained. "We don't hang out with the same people. I have no idea where I stand with you. It was easier for me just to arrange a way to run into you casually than get shot down by you if I called and asked you out. I just wasn't ready to risk the rejection."

Adrienne's eyebrows rose. Was Graydon actually admitting he had feelings? *Wow. First Cameron does her own homework, and now Graydon is acting like a regular, slightly shy guy. Has the entire world gone insane?*

"Okay, who are you and what have you done with the real Graydon Warner?" Adrienne demanded.

"You're one of the few people who has ever seen the real Graydon Warner," he said softly. Then he smirked his usual smirk. "And if you tell anyone that I actually admitted I have a fear of rejection, well, just remember I'm very well-connected. Those rumors about there being a Russian Mafia. . . ? You don't want to find out."

Adrienne laughed. Graydon was presumptuous, duplicitous, conniving, and right now utterly adorable.

"Oh, good!" Graydon said. "The lady laughs. So I'm guessing you won't mind when I invite myself upstairs."

"Are you kidding me?" Adrienne demanded, her hands on her hips. "You really like to push your luck, don't you?"

Graydon waggled his eyebrows at her. "Are you saying I could get lucky?"

Adrienne laughed and smacked his arm. For once his lecherous act really did seem like an act. *Maybe I've been oversensitive and he really has just been joking all along,* she thought.

He stood in the doorway looking at her. "Well. . . ?"

To Adrienne's shock, she was actually torn. But then sense took over. "I don't think my mom would appreciate just showing up with an extra person in time for dinner—which I'm already late for. Besides," she added, "if you want a date, you're going to have to actually ask me out. Not just horn in on a family meal."

Graydon shrugged. "Hey, I only wanted to meet your dad. I really want to take his macroeconomics class next year. This isn't actually about *you* at all." He shook his head. "Some girls are so egotistical."

"You are such a jerk," Adrienne said, laughing. She rummaged in her bag and pulled out her keys.

"And you are such a beauty," Graydon said. He reached out and brushed her bangs out of her eyes. Adrienne felt herself grow warm at his touch and, confused, took a step backward.

"So will you?" Graydon asked.

"Will I what?"

"Will you go out with me? You said I had to actually ask you, so I'm asking."

"Uh, o-okay," she said.

Graydon placed his hands on the wall behind her. He moved closer, and she raised her face to his.

Adrienne closed her eyes as she gave herself over to the kiss. His lips pressed against hers, and the feeling sent shivers of pleasure through her. She knew if she hadn't been leaning against the wall, she would have fallen over— her knees felt that wobbly.

Graydon pulled away. "Don't forget me," he said. "I know I'll be thinking about you." He grinned at her, then turned and climbed back into his Porsche.

Adrienne stayed leaning against the wall until he drove away. Luckily no one she knew had witnessed them kissing. She felt out of breath and exhilarated, her senses tingling. She had never felt that kind of intense chemistry with Brian.

She turned and went into her building. Could she have been wrong about him? Maybe he really did have this totally sweet, totally insecure side that just needed a girl he could trust to bring out.

It made her wonder: Maybe *she* was that girl?

CHAPTER SEVEN

horse sense

Liz put her heavy pile of books on the counter at the Salad Patch and placed her tiny Lulu Guinness purse on top of them. Now that spring was approaching, the girls of Pheasant-Berkeley had abandoned their backpacks in favor of the ridiculously small bags, and while, Liz admitted, the girls did look cute on Park Avenue clutching their tiny confections of grosgrain and silk, it had become difficult to travel without a larger bag for her textbooks.

None of her friends had arrived at the P–B hangout yet, but she was too hungry to wait. "Iced tea and a garden salad, please," Liz ordered as the waiter placed a glass of water and a set of silverware in front of her.

"And a porterhouse steak to go with that rabbit food," a familiar voice commented behind her.

Liz spun around on the chrome stool and saw Parker, hair disheveled and tie undone, standing behind her in the very sexy uniform of the boys at Dudley Academy: ripped jeans, oxford-cloth shirt, blue blazer, and expensive watch. The watch was, of course, optional, but it seemed that every boy at the tony private school sported a watch that cost as much as a small car on his wrist.

"Parker!" Liz said, slipping off the stool. Even though it had only been two days since she'd seen him, things had been strained at Jack Chasen's party, leaving Liz with a sour feeling. She was hoping to have a chance for some normal time with him, though she wasn't even sure what "normal" would mean at this point. He smiled a slow, sexy smile, slid his hands onto her hips, and kissed her.

Mmmmm, Liz thought. *That's better.*

Reassured by the playful affection of the kiss, she leaned away from him to see his face. "What's up? Why are you here? You guys out early?"

"Do I need a reason to come see my girl at lunch?" Parker moved his lips to her neck and nibbled.

"Well," Liz said, tingling with each soft bite, "since Dudley is across town, yes, you do!" She turned her face to kiss him again, then sat down. "But I'm happy to see you." She pushed her enormous pile of books aside to make room for Parker at the counter.

Parker hopped on the stool next to her and leaned in close, his shoulder touching hers.

"Actually," he said conspiratorially, "I'm ditching."

"The afternoon?" Liz said, eyes widening. "You'll be

so busted! They'll put you on probation, right?"

Parker shrugged. He took a swig from her water glass. "I may take off the whole week," he confessed.

Liz stared at him. *The whole week? He'll be expelled!* "You're not serious," she said.

"Yup." Parker glanced around the room, as if he suddenly realized they weren't alone. "Is anyone from P-B here?" he asked.

"Of course," Liz said. "You know we all hang out here. What's the problem?"

"This was a bad idea," Parker said, standing up. "Someone is going to see me and blab back at Dudley. I'd better take off. Call me later. I'll be hanging out in the park. Or downtown, or something. See you."

"Parker, wait!" Liz called as he hurried out the Salad Patch door, its bell jingling as it slammed behind him.

"Your order, miss." The man behind the counter placed a salad and iced tea in front of her, yanking her attention away from the door.

Liz stared down at the salad in front of her, but lunch was the farthest thing from her mind.

Liz arrived at the Claremont Riding Academy on West Eighty-ninth Street about ten minutes late. Her crosstown bus was stuck behind a limousine that seemed as if it would never move. When she got off the bus at

Columbus Avenue, Liz realized what had caused the hold-up: The limo contained a weeping Heather, a shouting David, and the inimitable Dr. Mayra Markham-Collins.

"Elizabeth!" Dr. M-C bellowed. The chauffeur holding open the door for her flinched but quickly recovered. "You're late!"

So are you, you big pain, Liz thought, but said, "Sorry!" instead, and ran down the block to meet them.

"Hi, Liz!" David said, jumping out of the car. "Heather is crying and she won't stop!"

Oh boy, Liz thought, *this will be great.*

"Elizabeth," Dr. M-C said, "I need to go inside and prepare the instructors for Heather's delicate psyche. They must be aware that they are dealing with an extraordinarily fragile child. Calm her down, then bring her inside. David, come with me." Dr. M-C strode into the old wooden building, David running to keep up with her.

The driver returned to the front seat, and Liz stuck her head into the car. Heather cowered in the corner of the backseat, a Hermès lap blanket over her head.

"Heather," Liz said gently, "are you all right?"

"I want to go home." Heather moaned from under the blanket. At least Liz was pretty sure that's what Heather said—her voice was muffled.

"Heather," Liz coaxed. "It's hard for me to hear you. Can you come out from under the blanket? Please?"

Heather sniffed. "I don't think so."

"Sure, you can," Liz encouraged her.

Heather pulled the blanket down from her face and looked at Liz with bleary, red-rimmed eyes. "Do I have to?"

Liz smoothed down Heather's hair. "Yeah, you do. Your mom is really into this."

Heather's lower lip quivered. "Have *you* ever ridden a horse?" she asked.

Liz's memory flashed back to a horrific ride at a fair, clutching the mane of a smelly, filthy horse that trotted too fast and made her sick to her stomach.

"Yes, I have," Liz said. "And, see! I survived." She gave Heather a broad grin.

Heather frowned, her furrowed brow making her look much older than her nine years. "Okay," she said reluctantly. "I'll go in. But I *won't* ride."

"That's fine," Liz said. "And your mom is going to be really proud of you."

Heather slid out of the limo, looking every inch the professional rider in her very expensive outfit. Except for the terrified look on her face, of course.

"I just hope I'm not permanently traumatized by this experience," Heather said shakily.

That goes for both of us, Liz thought. For the millionth time, Liz wondered how the renowned Dr. Markham-

Collins could be so completely clueless about her own kids.

Liz and Heather walked into the riding ring, which was open to the street. Heather planted her feet and refused to budge more than a few feet from the sidewalk.

Several young girls trotted in circles around the small dirt-covered ring. The animals were large and well-tended, their coats shining and clean. Liz admired the little girls who seemed to have no fear in spite of the fact that they were sitting on animals that could so easily throw or hurt them. Liz spotted David up in the tiny office, nose pressed to the window, mesmerized by the horses.

"Heels down!" an older man instructed one of the girls. "And, Caitlin, shoulders back! Look in the direction that you want to go—your mount needs to see you know what you're doing before she'll believe you're in control!"

Dr. M-C and David clattered down the steps from the office, followed by a trim woman in her forties. The woman beamed at Heather.

"Hello, Heather," she said. "My name is Alex-*ahn*-dra Winters," she said as if she were talking to a very small dog. "Your Mommy told me that you are a little scared of horses. Are you?"

"Heather is a *very* sensitive girl," Dr. M-C said, "and I think that some time with animals would do her good."

"Dr. Markham-Collins"— Ms. Winters turned to Dr.

M-C, her voice turning steely—"if your little girl needs time with *animals,* you should get her a kitten. If she wants to *ride,* then she should get up on a horse and work with me. I train champion equestrians, Doctor. I'm no babysitter. If Heather wants to commit to success, she can stay."

Dr. M-C blinked several times behind her black-rimmed glasses.

Whoa, Liz thought, *it looks like Dr. M-C has met her match. Way to go, Winters!*

Dr. M-C collected herself. "Heather *is* ready to succeed!" she declared. "Aren't you, Heather?"

Heather slipped behind Liz and clung to Liz's legs. Liz could feel the little girl's fingers trembling.

"Let's find Heather an appropriate horse," Ms. Winters said. "Jake!" She crossed to the side of the ring to confer with a young man wearing jeans and a sweatshirt. Dr. M-C and David trailed behind her.

"Okay, you can let go now, Heather." Liz twisted, trying to free herself from Heather's white-knuckled grip. Heather finally released Liz's now-bruised legs and stood there, quivering.

"It's not going to be that bad," Liz assured her. "Look at the other girls. They're having fun."

Heather glanced at the ring. The instructor brought the lesson to an end, and the girls dismounted, chatting happily as they led their horses to the stalls.

Heather went back to staring at her shiny new riding boots. "What if I get colic?" she whined.

"Get what?" Liz asked. She wasn't sure she had heard Heather correctly.

"Colic! I saw on a TV show that horses can get colic. And when Lindsay Cunningham's baby brother had colic, he screamed for hours and hours." Heather shuddered. "He was in *agony!*"

Liz shook her head. *It's true,* she mused, *a little knowledge is a dangerous thing.* "It's not the same kind of colic," she explained. In addition to being supersensitive, Heather could be a class-A hypochondriac. "Besides, it's not even contagious."

Heather looked at Liz dubiously, then she brightened. "What about hoof-and-mouth disease," she said. "Can I get that?"

"Heather, darling—look! They have a horse just for you!" Dr. M-C boomed from ringside.

Heather scurried behind Liz again.

Liz saw that Jake was leading a graying, slightly over-weight mare with soft brown eyes around into the ring. The horse looked extremely calm. In fact, Liz wondered if it was sleepwalking.

"See, Heather," Liz said, "this horse isn't scary at all."

Heather peeked out from behind Liz but made no move to the ring.

"Heather, you only *think* you are afraid," Dr. M-C lectured. "This is a false reality you have created. You aren't actually frightened, you only *believe* you are frightened, leading to your current need to act out as a scared child."

Everyone in the stable stared at Dr. M-C, clearly trying to make sense of the psychobabble. Even the horse looked perplexed.

"I want to ride!" David announced from where he was sitting in the dirt. "Let me!" He jumped back up.

Heather charged out from behind Liz and blocked David's path to the horse. "No!" she screeched at her little brother. "This is *my* riding lesson!"

Liz fought back a smile. *Nothing like a little sibling rivalry to motivate a kid.*

"Let's get started, then," Ms. Winters declared. "Heather, this horse's name is Mindreader."

Jake gave Heather a boost up while Ms. Winters explained how to mount the horse from the left and how to hold the reins between her thumbs and forefingers.

"Just sit up straight and feel the horse under you," she instructed. "That's right, you're doing fine!"

Heather sat bolt upright on Mindreader, her face white with terror.

That poor girl, Liz thought. *Why can't Dr. M-C see that this is pure torture for Heather?*

"She's got good posture," Ms. Winters commented.

"You can't teach that. I'll see you next Wednesday."

"Did you hear that, Heather? We're IN!" shouted Dr. M-C, as Heather sat pinned to Mindreader's back with fear. "Now try galloping around the ring, dear."

"She'll do no such thing!" Ms. Winters ordered. "Heather, do *not* give Mindreader that command!"

No danger of that, Liz thought. *The horse is the one in charge here. And I'm guessing Mindreader barely makes it above a trot on an energetic day.*

Liz was relieved to see that no matter how Dr. M-C may have exaggerated Heather's abilities, Ms. Winters saw right though it and chose a horse suited to Heather's temperament and *non*skill level.

A series of chimes caught Mindreader's attention. The horse shifted its weight and turned its large head toward the sound.

"Aghhhh!" Heather shrieked. She squeezed her eyes shut. "The horse is trying to eat me!"

"Oh, it's doing no such thing," Dr. M-C scolded, pulling out her cell phone—the source of the chimes. "Dr. Markham-Collins here."

"The horse just wanted to know who was on the phone," Liz called to Heather, who continued shrieking. "But if you keep screaming, you could make her mad."

Immediately Heather shut up. Now instead of white, her face was bright red. Liz was pretty sure Heather was holding her breath as a way to stop shouting.

"I have to go," Dr. M–C announced. "I'll leave you in Ms. Winters's capable hands. My client needs me. Her child was just rejected from the top nursery school in New York, and she is just devastated. Now that's a REAL problem."

Liz stared as Dr. M–C charged out of the stable as if she were on a true mission of mercy. She looked back at Heather, miserable on Mindreader, and sighed.

Doc, she thought, *you wouldn't know a real problem if it reared up and whinnied.*

CHAPTER EIGHT

what's normal?

Friday night Adrienne settled into a chair at a restaurant near the Warners' apartment on the Upper East Side. Bilboquet was a tiny French restaurant. The small tables were packed in tightly, and Adrienne realized that she was actually closer to the table next to her than she was to Graydon.

Graydon.

To Adrienne's complete and utter astonishment, every time they got together or spoke on the phone over the past two weeks, she discovered something about Graydon Warner that surprised and pleased her: his hope of creating a foundation to help disaster victims; the fact that he loved some of the same obscure black-and-white movies that she did; that he even shared her affection for old *Bewitched* reruns—an obsession that even Brian didn't know about and that she'd only recently confessed to Emma in a rare moment of nanny-mini-genius bonding.

"A bottle of Pol Roger, please," Graydon said to the

waiter, then fixed his dark eyes on Adrienne. "You like champ, right?"

"Sure," Adrienne said, barely able to hear him over the clamor of the young and attractive people around them. She glanced at the woman sitting at the next table.

She was blond and almost shockingly thin, dressed head to toe in Dior. A gorgeous aquamarine-and-diamond necklace glittered at her throat, and she chatted animatedly on her Vertu cell phone.

Five thousand dollars for a cell phone, Adrienne thought. *Can the reception actually be any better?* Judging by how loudly the woman was talking, it clearly wasn't. The woman fiddled with her glittering necklace absently as she chatted away about her couture fitting.

Adrienne gazed down at her own outfit. Though the Valentino cocktail dress was perfect for the evening, it felt like a hand-me-down compared with the clothes that the girls around her were wearing. Actually, it *was* a hand-me-down: one of Cameron's discards. She also appeared to be the only female on the premises who wore absolutely no jewelry. For the first time in a long time, Adrienne felt like a high school student playing dress-up.

Graydon grinned at her from across the table.

Adrienne blushed, feeling his unwavering, direct gaze. She ducked her head. "What?" she asked.

"I have something for you," he said. He reached into

his pocket and pulled out a tiny red leather box. Adrienne's eyes widened. She recognized the logo on the box—she'd seen similar ones in Mrs. Warner's jewelry collection. It was from the very expensive store Cartier.

I can't accept this, Adrienne's brain shouted. *It's too much.* "Graydon—" she began.

"I—I hope you like it," Graydon said, suddenly seeming nervous. "You might think it's kind of corny."

She couldn't imagine *anything* from Cartier being "corny." Curious, she took the box from him, opened it slowly, and gasped.

Nestled into the white satin fabric was a charm bracelet—but instead of the diamonds, rubies, and sapphires she had expected, the charms were made of chocolate!

"It's so cute!" Adrienne said, pulling the bracelet from the box. Each chocolate charm was wrapped in shiny colored tinfoil. She held and twisted the bracelet around so she could examine each adorable confection.

"Oh, good!" Graydon said with relief. "I saw them making the bracelets at this place over on Madison and thought you'd like one. But then I wasn't so sure . . ."

"I love it," Adrienne declared. "I just don't know if I want to eat it or keep it!"

Graydon suddenly looked worried. "You're not disappointed that it isn't from Cartier, are you? I just used a box I found at home."

Adrienne smiled. "This is *so* much better than some superexpensive rock."

"I'm really glad you like it." Graydon smiled shyly. "I—I want to get things right with you, Adrienne. You're different from the other girls I've known. So I—I just don't—"

"Menu?" interrupted the waiter. "Tonight we have . . ."

Graydon snapped back up. "Four ounces of beluga to start," he ordered in the pompous and familiar voice Adrienne recognized as the "old" Graydon.

"And for the young lady?" the waiter said.

"I'll have a hamburger," Adrienne said.

"A what?" the waiter replied, incredulous.

Graydon grinned. "Can the fish eggs," he said. "Make that two hamburgers."

"Medium rare," Adrienne said.

"With *onions,*" Graydon added.

"And pickles . . ."

"And ketchup . . ."

"And fries . . ."

"And would you like shakes with that?" the waiter asked, his voice dripping with sarcasm. "Monsieur Warner, this is Bilboquet, *not* McDonald's." He shuddered.

"Can you make a hamburger or not?" Graydon asked.

"The best in New York, sir," the waiter replied, "but . . ."

"Then two hamburgers, please," Graydon said. "And

cancel the champagne. I want a Coke."

"Me, too!" Adrienne called as the waiter quickly left, exasperated.

Graydon looked at Adrienne, shook his head, and grinned. "You really are too much," he said.

"You know, Graydon, I really thought I knew you," Adrienne said. "That you were the biggest player around. But you know what? I think underneath all the loud game, there's a really nice guy who just wants to be normal."

"What's normal?" Graydon asked, laughing.

"Well, Gray, if you don't know, it's too late for you," Adrienne teased. "But I can tell you this: normal *isn't* a three-hundred-dollar bottle of champagne on a date with a girl who works as a nanny and goes to a public school."

"You're more than that, Adrienne," Graydon said.

"Am I?" Adrienne asked. "I need you to be straight with me." She looked him in the eye. "What are we doing? Where is this going?"

Graydon reached across the table and took both of Adrienne's hands in his. His hands felt strong and warm.

"I'd like it to go further," he said.

"I'm not sure *your* idea of further is where I want to go," Adrienne said quietly.

Graydon released her hands and leaned back in his chair. He cocked his head as if he were studying her. "Sounds like my reputation has preceded me," he said.

Adrienne shrugged. "People talk."

"People *lie!*" Graydon said, suddenly angry.

"Hey, hey!" Adrienne said, startled by his reaction. "I didn't mean to hurt your feelings, I just heard—"

"I know what you heard," Graydon said bitterly. "You heard that I cheated on every girl I ever dated. You heard that Serena Bedford tried to kill herself after we broke up. You heard that I flew Lydia Stetson to Bermuda to be with me but then got her out of the way by shipping her off to Hilton Head so I could sleep with Jane Tauber. . . ." His voice trailed off, and he glared down at the table.

"It was Santa Fe," Adrienne said. "I heard you shipped Lydia to Santa Fe. You really need to keep better track of your scandals."

Graydon's eyes flicked up and searched her face. When he realized that she was joking, his eyes crinkled and the two of them burst into outrageous laughter.

"Your *hamburgers,*" the waiter announced with disgust.

"Thank you," Graydon said, choking as he tried to catch his breath.

Adrienne delicately touched the napkin to her eye. She laughed so hard, her eyes actually welled up with tears. She hoped she hadn't smeared her mascara.

When the waiter left the table, Graydon grew serious again. "Adrienne, I'm not going to lie to you. I—I haven't always been a stand-up guy, but I don't want to be that way with you. And yes, I've been with my share of girls. Maybe more than my share. But a lot of what you hear is just gossip—and seriously exaggerated."

"Okay," Adrienne said, wanting to believe him. She'd seen firsthand how gossip could spin out of control.

"And one of the reasons I acted like a player was that I never really cared enough about any of those girls to do it any different. With the right girl . . ." His voice trailed off again and Graydon looked down at his plate.

Adrienne's green eyes widened, and she could feel her heart thump a little harder. *Wow*, she thought, *he really does seem to want to make this work.*

"Let's just keep seeing how things go," Adrienne said, hoping she sounded mature and cool. She was pleased by how relieved Graydon looked.

"I don't know about you," she added, "but I'm starving. Let's eat these burgers before they get cold."

"Good idea," Graydon said. "If we sent them back, I think the waiter would personally pay to have us executed."

CHAPTER NINE

Parker's big secret

When Adrienne arrived at the Warners' apartment Monday after school, she found Emma in the huge kitchen, the round table in front of her a mess of wires and switches.

"What are you doing?" Adrienne asked.

"I'm convinced that Kane is stealing from Cameron," the little girl replied. "So I am laying a trap in her room."

Adrienne raised her eyebrows. *What would Kane swipe from Cam?* she thought. *Size 0 Prada pants?*

"She is make me crazy," said Tania. "All with this fiddle-fiddle. I find camera in closet, microphone in refrigerator."

"Tania talks to the food in Russian," Emma said, giggling.

"I talk to *self*!" Tania exclaimed, throwing her hands up. "I talk about dinner! I talk about crazy little girl should be playing with dolls and not playing KGB agent! *Gospodi pomilui!*" She left the kitchen, muttering a long stream of Russian that Adrienne assumed was about Emma.

"I thought I told you no more video," Adrienne scolded Emma.

Emma looked up at her with a completely innocent expression. "I thought you meant I couldn't have the camera in front of the hallway powder room."

"Emma—" Adrienne began.

Cameron strode in. "Hello, freakling," she greeted Emma, dropping her miniature Hermés Kelly bag on the table right on top of Emma's technical manual. She grabbed a bottle of designer water from the Sub-Zero fridge.

"Cameron," Emma said, tossing the Hermés bag to the floor, "if you existed—which you don't—I'd still ignore you."

"Isn't she darling?" Cameron yanked a wire out of place as she crossed the room. She pointed the pale blue bottle of water at Adrienne. "You, however, are a gift from heaven." Cameron fixed her dazzling approximation of a smile on Adrienne. "Follow me!" Cameron turned and went back out to the living room, swooping up her bag on the way out.

This is going to be bad, Adrienne thought. "I'll be right back," she told Emma.

Adrienne stepped into the huge living room, where Cameron was lounging on the suede-covered sofa. Cameron patted the seat next to her. "Come sit by me, Adrienne. Time for a little girl-talk."

Adrienne crossed the Italian-tiled floor and sat down hesitantly. Cameron was a snake, but now that she was seeing Graydon, Adrienne felt she should try to get along with her a little better. Cameron not only was Graydon's half sister, she was an expert at making trouble—something Adrienne really wanted to avoid.

Cameron took a swig of her water, then faced Adrienne. "So, as you know, it is my current mission to have Mimi deposed from her position as chair of the Young Lions Committee of the Library."

Adrienne nodded. She didn't understand *why* it was such an obsession with Cam, just that it was a major one. *Probably because Cam can't stand losing,* Adrienne realized.

"Well, this week we had our history essay contest, and we all had to hand in our disks with the essays today."

Adrienne nodded, wondering where Cam was going with this and what any of it had to do with the library. Or with her.

"It's a pity that Mimi didn't hand hers in."

"She didn't submit her disk?" Adrienne asked, surprised. From what she had seen, Mimi was no airhead.

Cameron giggled. "Not exactly. She submitted a disk all right. A disk with a really lousy essay that begins 'Kings are good. My grandfather was a king. I think kings are really cool with their awesome castles and everything. . . . '"

Adrienne's mouth dropped open. Cam had switched

essays on Mimi? So this was the reason Cameron had developed a sudden interest in homework.

"Pretty brilliant, yes?" Cameron smiled.

"I don't see what any of this has to do with me," Adrienne said.

"I'm getting to that," Cameron said.

Adrienne braced herself.

"I want you to make an anonymous call to the library."

"Saying?" Now Adrienne was even more confused. This was getting weirder by the minute.

"Saying that it is a scandal that Princess Mimi von Fallschirm is the chair of the Young Lions Committee of the Library when she is barely literate. And you have the failing essay to prove it!"

Adrienne stared at Cameron. *Unbelievable.* She knew Cameron was a shallow, duplicitous bitch. But to go this far? Just to be head of some stupid committee?

"No way," Adrienne said.

"What did you say?" Cameron said, tilting her head and gazing at Adrienne. "Sorry, darling, that almost actually sounded like 'no.'"

"I won't do it."

"Oh yes, you will," Cameron said, her voice hard. "And then you will follow up that phone call with another one to Page Six of the *New York Post*."

This is just so mean! Adrienne thought. *And Mimi is supposedly one of Cam's best friends.*

Adrienne stood. "Sorry, Cam."

"You *will* be sorry," Cameron warned. She stretched her long, slim legs, then stood. "I will make very certain that you're sorry. Gee, I wonder what your pal Liz will think when she finds out that you had the chance to help her but you didn't?"

"What are you talking about?" Adrienne demanded.

"I have info on Parker. Shocking info, if I must say so myself." Cameron smiled secretly. "You help me. I help Liz."

Adrienne stared at Cameron. She knew all too well how skilled Cameron was at twisting things. She didn't think Liz would actually believe anything Cam said, but still. . . .

And if Cam was the key to helping Liz with Parker, then how could Adrienne say no?

But how could she say yes?

"Do your own dirty work, Cameron," Adrienne said.

She thought she saw a flicker of shock appear and quickly vanish as Cameron kept her icy eyes fixed on her. Adrienne held her breath, wondering what Cameron might do. After what seemed like forever, Cameron shrugged. "Do what you like, Adrienne, that's fine."

Adrienne tried not to show her incredible surprise

that Cameron was actually backing down.

"But there is something you *can* do, if it doesn't offend your sensibilities," Cameron said.

Okay, here it comes, Adrienne thought.

"Lend me your cell," Cameron said.

Adrienne stared at Cameron, confused. "Why? Isn't yours working?"

"Discretion, sweetie," Cameron explained. "I can't have my personal number turning up in any caller IDs."

"And it's all right if *my* number shows up?" Adrienne asked.

"Hate to break this to you, but no one knows who you are. Your number is on no one's radar." Cameron held out her hand, waiting for Adrienne to cough up the phone.

"I'll give it to you," Adrienne said, "but only if you tell me what you know about Parker."

Cameron cocked her head and looked at Adrienne. "I guess fair's fair," she said. "I did promise to tell you the juicy little secret. I just hope you and your goody-two-shoes friend can handle it."

"Just spill it." Adrienne was getting impatient. "What is going on with Parker?"

"Come *on*, Adrienne," Cameron said, exasperated. "You and your friend Liz can't tell what Parker is doing?"

Adrienne shook her head.

Cameron rolled her eyes and sighed. "Adrienne," she

said as if Adrienne were a small child. "Parker Devlin is dealing."

"Dealing? You mean, dealing *drugs?*" Adrienne was stunned.

Cameron nodded and smiled.

"You're not serious?" she asked.

"Serious as a felony," Cameron said.

"Who is he dealing drugs to? The kids at his school? Your school?" Adrienne demanded, trying to process this revelation.

"Who do you think the private school kids get their drugs from?" Cameron smirked. "Your friend Liz should dump him and fast if she wants to keep that squeaky clean rep of hers. Though I suppose just hanging out with him this long has already done some damage. Guilt by association, you know. And you can tell her that I said that as a friend."

There is nothing friendly about you, Cameron, Adrienne thought.

Cameron snapped her fingers. "Phone. Now."

Adrienne stared at Cameron, a sick feeling welling up inside her as she fumbled in her purse for her phone.

How am I going to tell Liz? Adrienne wondered.

CHAPTER TEN

I know the truth

Liz's hand shook as she clicked off her cell phone. All through the conversation with Adrienne, Liz's mind had been spinning. Now she was having trouble breathing.

Is it really true? she wondered.

She perched on the edge of her bed, elbows on her knees, head in her hands. She kept hearing Adrienne's voice repeating the terrible sentence: "He's selling drugs."

"No!" Liz stood and paced the room. She refused to believe it. Sure, Parker got high now and then, but to actually be selling the stuff? That would make him really low.

But still . . . She sat down hard on her desk chair. It explained so much. The constant phone calls, the disappearing acts, the erratic behavior.

She felt herself grow cold as Adrienne's revelation about Parker made more and more sense. Now that she thought about it, it had been totally obvious from day one. No wonder Cameron thought she and Adrienne were naive little girls. All the signs were right there, but she had been too starry-eyed to see them.

She smacked herself on the forehead. "I am such an idiot! How could I have not seen it?"

"Liz?"

Liz froze at her mother's knock on her door.

"I can hear you talking," her mom said. "Tell whoever you're on the phone with good night and get ready for bed."

"O-okay, Mom," Liz said, hoping her voice didn't betray her emotional state. There was no way she could talk to her mom about this. *She'd forbid me to ever see Parker again.*

But isn't that exactly what I should do? Liz thought. *How can I keep going out with him knowing this?*

She stretched out on her bed and stared at the ceiling. She knew there'd be no way she'd be getting any sleep tonight.

The next day Liz covered the dark circles under her eyes the best she could and then forced herself through the heavy scarlet door of the Pheasant-Berkeley School for Girls.

Liz assumed the day would be complete hell. Cameron had probably already spread it around that Liz was such an unsophisticated twerp, she didn't even know her own boyfriend was dealing.

As Liz walked through the halls, she tried to put a brave face on, smiling at friends and acquaintances and holding her head high as she passed a knowing-looking Cameron and a smug Isabelle Schuyler.

"Have a nice night, Liz?" Cameron cooed. "Learn anything new?"

"Only to mind my own business, Cameron," she said. She turned to walk away.

"But did you hear the news?" Cameron asked, her voice ripe with suggestion.

Liz knew she should just keep walking, but she turned anyway. "You seem to have a lot of information for other people, Cameron."

"I know!" Cameron said. "I'm like CNN—Cameron News Network! I should talk to Parker about putting me on TV. Oh wait, Parker's a little busy with his own ventures right now, isn't he, Liz?"

Isabelle giggled.

Well, there's my answer right there, Liz thought. *Everyone knows, and they've been laughing behind my back all this time!*

"But the real breaking story on the Cameron News Network has nothing to do with you and Parker," Cameron said. "Have you noticed that Mimi isn't in school today?"

"Do I really care, Cameron?" Liz asked, desperate to get away.

"Look at this." Cameron thrust a newspaper at Liz. "Can you *believe* it?"

Liz glanced down at the paper. It was Page Six of the *New York Post*. Liz skimmed the gossip column filled with boldfaced names until she reached a section carefully circled in pink ink:

CROWNED AIRHEAD ROLLS AT LIBRARY

It seems that Debutante of the Year **Princess Mimi von Fallschirm** has suffered a serious social setback. An anonymous call to the New York Public Library has alerted trustees to the fact that the new chair of the exclusive "Young Lions" benefit can barely write, let alone read the books on the library's shelves. Sources at the NYPL reveal the board is seeking a more literate "Lioness" to head this season's benefit. Hey, **Mimi**! How about getting hooked on phonics?

"Can you *believe* it?" Cameron asked, taking back the paper and smiling down at it. "Poor, poor Mimi. How *humiliating* for her!"

"She must be totally wrecked," Isabelle agreed.

"I feel terrible for her," Cameron continued as girls began to gather around her and peer at the newspaper, which Cameron just happened to keep waving. "We must all be very supportive of her in her time of need."

"You are such a good friend," Isabelle gushed. "You know, Cameron, you were totally the other contender for Deb of the Year. They should ask you to replace her as committee head."

"Isabelle, that's sweet of you to say," Cameron said in a voice that indicated her response had been carefully rehearsed. "But I'm very busy with my other charities. If the library asked me, I'd be honored, of course, but really, the kids need me."

"Which kids, Cameron?" Isabelle asked in the same artificial voice, designed to be overheard by the girls who were clustering around Cameron, excited by Mimi's demise.

"Why, the kids at the Warner Center of Columbia Presbyterian Hospital, of course. Kids without the chances that my brother, my sister, and I have had over the years. It is my obligation and my privilege to be able to help those amazing little children."

Oh, my God, Liz thought, nauseated by the display. *Cameron will totally win the Oscar for her role as someone who cares.*

"But really," Cameron said, "my heart is *breaking* for Mimi. She doesn't deserve this kind of treatment in the press. I'm going to see her tonight to find out if there's anything I can do. She is beside herself over this, and all the papers are trying to get a shot of her looking miserable. It's so unfair."

"You're, like, a saint, Cameron," Isabelle said. "To stick by Mimi in the middle of all this."

"Isabelle," Cameron said, smiling. "What are friends for?"

With friends like Cam, who needs serial killers, Liz thought, walking away from the group of gossiping girls. The one good thing about the whole mess with Mimi was that it seemed to be taking up most of Cameron's attention. Which meant she'd leave Liz and Parker alone. Maybe even long enough for Liz to figure out what to do.

After school, Liz watched Heather walk slowly around the circle on Mindreader, her face contorted in an expression of agony. Poor Heather had faced the inevitable and didn't protest the lessons anymore. At least not at home. Still, four lessons in and the little girl hadn't shown any improvement—in technique or in attitude.

"Shoulders back!" Ms. Winters shouted. "Keep your heels down!"

Heather's lip quivered, and Mindreader stared blankly ahead.

"Good!" Ms. Winters said. "Now, we're going to trot a bit. When we trot, we do something we call *posting.* When we post, we lift ourselves out of the saddle just a little bit as the horse moves. That way, we don't bounce around in our seat. Ready?"

Ms. Winters clicked her tongue, and Mindreader picked up the pace. Heather bounced wildly in the saddle, her voice breaking every time she smashed back down in the saddle.

"L-IZ, I c-AN'T d-O th-IS any-MORE!" Heather wailed as Mindreader blithely trotted around the circle. "I WANT to STOP! NOW!"

"Let's take a break," Ms. Winters said, exasperated. "She'll have to get over these hurdles and adjust her attitude or she'll never move on."

"Yes, Ms. Winters," Liz said. "I'll have a talk with her."

"If you think it will help," Ms. Winters said. "Do what you can."

Heather dismounted and stumbled toward Liz, who was leaning against the wall of the office.

"I want to go home," Heather complained.

"Come on, Heather," Liz said. "I know you can do it!" She turned Heather to face the ring and put her arm around her. "Mindreader isn't so bad. She really seems to be taking to you, and you look good on her."

"I do?" Heather said.

"Sure you do! You just have to be a little less afraid. Do you think Mindreader wants you flopping around on her back like a sack of potatoes?"

"I guess not," Heather said.

"I think if you stop being so afraid, you'll be able to

understand the instructions better. It's normal to be scared of new things. But you'll feel so much better if you face what you're afraid of head–on and don't give up."

Heather bit her lip as if she were considering what Liz was saying.

Whaddya know, Liz thought. *My pep talk might actually be working.* She didn't want to lose momentum now.

"And you know what? Afterward, you might not even remember why you thought it was so scary in the first place."

"I don't know. . . ."

"Ready to take another shot?"

"Oh, all right," Heather said.

"Ready?" Ms. Winters called once Heather had climbed back up onto Mindreader.

"Ready," Heather said, her voice a bit more confident.

I should listen to my own advice, Liz realized. *I'm so afraid of talking to Parker that I'm making it even worse.*

Liz decided she would track Parker down tonight and have it out with him. *I just hope that I mean enough to him,* she thought, *to get him to stop.*

Liz walked into JG Melon's on Third Avenue. The hamburger shop and bar was a hangout for the boys at Dudley, and Parker and the swim team regularly had dinner there after practice on Thursdays.

She really hated barging in, but she didn't know what else to do. For the last four days she had phoned, e-mailed, and texted, and Parker hadn't replied. He was back in elusive mode. But she knew she had to have this conversation *tonight*. She was *not* going to spend another horrible night tossing and turning, running every scenario she could think of and generally making herself insane.

Liz walked in and looked around the wood-paneled room. She spotted Parker's friends sitting around one of the red-checked-cloth covered tables in the back.

"Hey, guys," Liz said, stepping up to the table.

"Hey, Liz," said Jack Chasen. "You meeting some other lovelies from P-B?"

"Actually, no," Liz said. "I'm looking for Parker."

"Oh." Jack frowned, then glanced at the other guys at the table.

Liz suddenly felt super self-conscious. She started worrying that this had been a very bad idea.

No, she told herself. *This has to be done, and done now.*

"Parker was out of school today," Jack said, looking around the table. "We don't think he's even coming."

"What, and miss treating my favorite scoundrels to burgers?"

Liz turned to see Parker standing behind her, gorgeous as ever. He looked surprised when he realized that it was Liz who was standing in front of him.

"Hey Liz, what are you doing here?" he asked.

Liz blushed, knowing the entire table was watching them. She stepped in closer. "I-I really need to talk to you," she said quietly.

"Guys, I'll be right back." He took Liz by the arm and led her through the restaurant back out onto Third Avenue.

"Liz, what's wrong? What's so important that you came here tonight? I thought you understood about boys' night."

Liz took a deep breath. "Parker," she said in a low voice. "I know."

"About what?" Parker asked.

"About the drugs," Liz whispered. She didn't want any of the passersby on the sidewalk to hear her.

"So?" he said.

Liz stepped back and stared up at him. "*So,* Parker," she said. "You could get into trouble. You could go to *jail.*"

"For getting high every once in a while?" he asked, amused. He snickered. "They'd have to arrest every kid in every private school in New York if that were a real problem."

"Parker," Liz said firmly, "not every kid in every private school in New York is dealing drugs."

Parker's expression went from amused to dumbfounded. "I don't deal drugs," he said. "Liz, *poor* kids deal drugs. I have more money than any kid in New York, and you, of all people, should know that."

"But the phone calls, the running around . . ." Liz faltered. This conversation was going very differently from how she had expected.

"Damn, Liz, I'm popular, for christsakes." Parker sighed. "I am *not* dealing drugs. I'm too rich and too smart for that, and you know it. I'm not a stoner—you know that, too." He rubbed his face, then looked straight at her. "Honestly, Liz. You have to trust me on this one." Parker gave Liz a quick peck on the cheek and went back into Melon's.

Liz stood in the fading light, staring at the spot where her boyfriend had just been.

Either he's telling the truth, Liz thought, *or he's in serious denial.*

And I'm left exactly where I was before: absolutely, totally confused.

CHAPTER ELEVEN

and it only gets better

Saturday evening Adrienne gazed down at Manhattan, spread out below her like a carpet of lights.

"Gorgeous, isn't it?" Graydon asked, leaning across her to peer through the airplane's curtained window. Then he swiveled in the plush, adjustable chair so that he could face her. "Just like you."

He pressed his lips against hers, and Adrienne's heart fluttered. She pulled him even closer, letting his kiss sweep over her.

When Graydon had called and suggested grabbing a bite out of town, he hadn't been kidding. This time, though, she didn't panic the way she had on their first date. Now she felt willing to go pretty much anywhere with Graydon. He had proved on every date that he could be trusted—that his sleazy, grabby ways were part of the past.

A quick ride in the Rolls to the airport had put them on the Warners' jet. Adrienne had been on the plane before, when she went with the family for nanny duty in Palm Beach; but she was not prepared for what it was like when it was just her, Graydon, and the endless stars that were just appearing.

"Mmmmm," Graydon murmured as he pulled away from her. "You sure are tasty." He reached for the bottle of designer water that sat chilling on a mahogany side table. "Want something to drink?"

"Thanks," she said. She couldn't stop looking at him as he poured the sparkling water into crystal flutes and handed her one. *He is soooooooo good-looking*, she thought.

"To getting to know each other better and better," Graydon said. He clinked her glass.

Adrienne took a sip and gazed around the airplane cabin. The walls were covered in silk brocade, and in one corner there was a small piano just in case Emma might need to practice while airborne. The in-flight blankets were Hermès, and the snacks were catered by one of Jean-Georges's many white-hot restaurants.

"Whatcha thinking?" Graydon asked.

Adrienne smiled. "Just thinking how weird it is to be here."

Graydon looked at her quizzically. "Should I be insulted?"

"No," Adrienne said with a laugh. "I don't mean it's weird to be with you—though, actually, come to think of it, if you had told me a month ago that I'd be on a date with you . . ."

"Voluntarily," Graydon said with a smirk.

"Exactly," Adrienne said, laughing, "and that I'd be enjoying myself?" She shrugged. "Let's just say that this is *not* what I would have been predicting."

Graydon moved closer to her. "Do you mean that? That you're enjoying yourself?"

"Of course," Adrienne said. It melted her a little every time he revealed just how vulnerable he could be. "Don't I seem like I'm enjoying myself?"

"I guess . . ." Graydon kissed her again, and she made sure he knew just how much fun she was having. They broke apart, and Graydon leaned back against his upholstered seat. "Okay. *Now* I believe that you're enjoying yourself."

Adrienne giggled, a little embarrassed by how much she had led that make-out moment.

Graydon looked at his watch. "It's almost eight. We're practically there." He picked up the phone, which connected him to the cockpit. "Paul? Gray here. Is the car waiting? Cool. We're landing now?"

Adrienne looked out the window. There was water everywhere.

"Uh, Graydon," Adrienne said. "Where are we?"

"That's Baltimore," Graydon replied. "I know a great little place for crab cakes there."

Baltimore. As in Maryland. A grin snaked across Adrienne's face. *I can't believe that this is even my life!*

"Take a look at this!" Cameron Warner said Sunday morning. She tossed a copy of *The New York Times* on the kitchen table between Emma and Adrienne. "Blake Weinstein is a total genius!"

Adrienne turned, bleary-eyed. The COW had called waaaay too early that morning begging, pleading, and basically ordering Adrienne to come in on a Sunday. Reluctantly, Adrienne agreed—it was easier than arguing, and Mrs. Warner promised to double the rate for the day. But Adrienne had eaten too many crab cakes and hadn't gotten home until 1 A.M., and her parents had been furious!

They'd have killed me if they knew I was out of the state! Adrienne thought. *No, first they would have killed Graydon.* Then *they would have killed me.*

"What, Cam?" she replied.

"Don't encourage her," Emma grumbled. She took a spoonful of cereal. That was all Adrienne had managed to come up with as breakfast. Tania had some family emergency, though Adrienne wondered if maybe the emergency was that Tania just had to get away from this crazy family.

Cameron whacked Emma on the head with her purse.

"Hey!" Emma yelped.

"Okay, Cameron, I'll play," Adrienne said. She hoped once Cam got the attention she needed, she'd go away. "Who is Blake Weinstein, and why is he a genius?"

"He is my new PR guy," Cameron said. "When I was using Gabby Litsman, all I got was bad press. Well, duh, she was, like, thirty, and totally jealous of me. But Blake is fabulous!"

Adrienne looked down at the newspaper. "WARNER SIBLINGS LEARN PHILANTHROPY EARLY," the headline said. Below it was a photograph of Cameron and Graydon sitting on tiny chairs, reading a book aloud to a group of rapt and adorable children.

Cameron dropped onto a chair. "Read it out loud, won't you? I just love hearing the words of a true literary talent."

"'Cameron Warner,'" Adrienne read aloud, "'has followed the example of her stepmother Christine Olivia Warner, a known New York socialite and philanthropist. Since her stunning debut at the recent Manhattan Cotillion, Miss Warner has spent more time at the library, and less time dancing on tabletops.'"

"Fabulous, no?" Cameron said, rummaging in her purse. "Go on."

"'"I just think that I've grown out of my bad-girl days," Warner says, her famously silver-blue eyes downcast. "The future of New York is in its kids, and I'm lucky to be able to help the library increase literacy."'"

Adrienne lowered the paper and stared at Cameron. "Are you really working with kids in a literacy program?"

"Well, that day I was, sure," Cameron said, checking her lip gloss in a gilded pocket mirror. "Blake set the whole thing up."

Emma looked up from her copy of *Surreptitious Sonic Engineering* magazine. "Cameron," she asked, "can you even read?"

"Shut up, ratbag." Cameron snapped her compact shut. "I read *Vogue* cover to cover every month, and in September, that's, like, *a thousand* pages."

Emma snorted.

"Go on, it gets better," Cameron instructed Adrienne.

" 'With Graydon and Cameron Warner as the new co-chairs of the Young Lions' Committee for Development, the city will certainly be a better place because of their efforts.' "

"So Mimi's out, and you and Graydon are in." Adrienne put down the newspaper. "You got what you wanted."

"Don't I always?" Cameron stood. "Well, I'll leave you to . . . well, whatever it is that you do." She picked up the newspaper and headed for the door. She stopped and turned.

"You know, Adrienne, at first I wasn't all that happy that I'd have to share the committee with Graydon," she said.

I'm not surprised, Adrienne thought. Sharing was definitely not high on the list of Cameron's skills. "Oh?"

"But thanks to you, he seems to have actually become a human. I don't know what you're doing, but keep it up. He's so much easier to deal with now." She left the room, leaving behind the faint scent of Joy.

"What do you think it would take to make *Cameron* human?" Adrienne asked.

"If you figure it out, please let me be the first to know," Emma said.

Liz stood in Dr. M-C's kitchen, locked in mortal combat with David over a plate of eggplant and soy cakes from the trendy veggie restaurant Zen Palate. Heather had dutifully finished her dinner and had been allowed to go to her room to play.

"I won't!" David shouted.

"If you eat all of this, I *promise* I will give you a Twinkie," Liz coaxed.

"No," David said.

"Cheez Doodles," Liz tried.

"No," David said.

"Hostess Cupcakes?"

David paused. "Snowballs?" he asked.

"Done. Eat the eggplant."

David dug into his meal.

Victory! Liz thought.

Her cell phone rang. She checked the caller ID, hoping it was Parker. She hadn't heard from him after their weird conversation at JG Melon three nights ago. No such luck—it was Adrienne.

Well, she thought, clicking on the phone, *maybe Adrienne can help me figure out what my next move with Parker should be.*

"Turn on the TV!" Adrienne shouted.

"What?" Liz said, wondering why Adrienne sounded so frantic.

"I'm telling you to turn on the TV!" Adrienne shrieked. "CNN!"

"Uh, okay." Liz got up and went out to the living room and clicked the remote.

". . . and as we promised, more on the breaking news from Madison Avenue," said the blond newscaster. "Media mogul Reed Devlin was escorted out of his offices today under indictment for a financial scandal in which he was implicated. . . ."

Liz stared at the screen in horror. There, in high definition for all the world to see, was the unmistakable figure of Parker Devlin's father.

In handcuffs.

CHAPTER TWELVE

totally MIA

Oh my God, Liz thought, staring at the screen. *What is going on?*

Liz forced herself to pay attention to the anchorwoman, but she was so freaked out, she had trouble following the story. Words like "insider trading," "mismanaged funds," and even "embezzlement" were tossed around. The more Liz listened, the worse the story seemed to get.

Parker! I have to talk to Parker. He needs me!

She dropped the remote and raced to the door.

"Liz?" a voice behind her stopped her. She turned and saw David.

"You promised me Snowballs!" David said in an accusing tone. "I ate the eggplant."

"What? Oh, right." *You are completely losing it!* she scolded herself. *You can't just run out on your job.* She forced herself to calm down and return to earth.

"Let's go back in the kitchen," Liz said. "We don't want your mom to know about our deal, right?"

Dr. M–C was seriously anti–junk food, which was why the treats were such effective tools for bribery.

David grinned. "Right!"

He turned and went back into the kitchen. Following him, Liz passed the TV and saw that the newscaster had moved on to another story. She clicked off the set and started counting the minutes to when she could leave and talk to Parker.

David and Heather had kept Liz thoroughly occupied, so other than leaving a quick message on Parker's voice mail, she had had no contact with him. She hoped now that she was home, she'd be able to really talk to him.

As she shut the door to the apartment behind her, Liz heard the TV blaring in the living room.

"Liz?" her mother called, "is that you?"

"Uh, yeah," Liz responded, praying that she could get into her room and escape to call Parker. She didn't want to waste another minute.

"Come in and talk to me," her mom called.

Liz's shoulders sagged, but there was no way to fend off her mom. She had the feeling her mother had also seen the news and wanted to talk to her about it.

She stepped into the living room. It was a lot messier than Dr. M–C's, with books, magazines, and papers scattered around. It was also a lot less fancy, decorated with sale items from Bed Bath & Beyond, rather than by high-priced designers. But it was also a lot more comfortable to live in.

Her mom was sitting on the worn sofa, a soft blanket pulled over her. Liz had gotten her dark hair and eyes from her mom, but definitely not her height. Her dad towered over her petite mom, and so did Liz.

"Are you okay?" Liz's mom asked, deep furrows appearing in her forehead.

"I guess," Liz said, plopping down beside her mother. "So I suppose you heard the news?"

Her mom patted Liz's knee. "I'm afraid by now everyone has heard the news. How is Parker?"

"I don't know," Liz said. "I haven't had a chance to talk to him yet."

Ms. Braun nodded. "This is going to be hard on him." She shook her head angrily. "Mr. Devlin is astoundingly selfish!"

"What do you mean?" Liz asked.

"As if he wasn't already rich enough," her mom ranted. "Not only does he pilfer his own employees' retirement funds, he does so with no regard for what might happen to his family if he got caught. The arrogance!"

"It's a mistake," Liz protested. She hated thinking Mr. Devlin would do anything so awful. She hoped for Parker's sake that it was all just a horrible misunderstanding. "Besides, isn't he innocent until proven guilty?"

Her mother's anger faded and was replaced with a look of sympathy. "You're absolutely right. But I do want you to be aware that there is going to be a *lot* of gossip about this at school. And about Parker."

"I know," Liz moaned. "This is going to wreck Parker."

"I worry how that's going to affect you," her mom said, her face serious.

"All I care about is Parker," Liz said.

"I know, honey. You're a good friend. Believe me, Parker is going to need one."

Liz stood up. "I want to try calling again, okay?"

"Okay," her mother replied. "Hang in there."

Liz went to her room and tried Parker on his cell, and at home. No answer.

Liz hung up and sent a quick e-mail. She looked at her buddy list—Parker wasn't online.

Liz lay on her bed and stared at her phone. *Please call me, Parker.*

She woke up in the dark, still dressed, still facing the phone. The phone that never rang.

"So, my father says that the Devlins are ruined," Cameron announced at lunch to Isabelle Schuyler.

Liz hated that her friends had sat near Cameron, but all the other tables had already been snapped up. She wished she had gone to the Salad Patch, but Jane and

Belinda had some project they were working on and didn't want to take the time to go off-campus. Liz couldn't figure out why Cameron was eating in the cafeteria, since she hardly ever did. *Of course,* Liz realized, *gossip is much more satisfying with an audience.*

"It's so sad," Isabelle said. "Parker is really nice."

"Well, now he's also really poor," Cameron said with a smirk. "I heard that their assets are frozen while all of their financial dealings are scrutinized."

Isabelle gasped. "I'd hate that! I don't want *anyone* seeing where I use my credit card."

"And now that information is going to be splashed all over the news," Cameron said with malicious glee. She raked her fingers through her perfect hair and cocked her head. "This is *so* much juicer than Parker's drug dealing."

Isabelle looked at Cameron with surprise. "I never heard that Parker was selling drugs. And I think I'd *know.*"

Cameron's brow furrowed. "I guess I got my facts wrong." She shot a smug look at Liz.

Liz's jaw dropped. "You what?" she said to Cameron.

Jane put her hand over Liz's. "Stay cool," she warned quietly. "Don't let her get to you."

Cameron looked at Liz as if she were having trouble placing her. "Oh, Liz. I'm sorry. Obviously your little friend Adrienne has been gossiping. And obviously *you* are ready to believe the worst of your boyfriend."

"Down, girl," Jane murmured to Liz. "Keep it together."

Liz forced herself to turn away.

"Come to think of it, though," Cameron continued, "maybe he WILL start dealing. He'll certainly need the money now."

Liz fumed so hard that she thought smoke *had* to be coming out of her ears. Any minute the top of her head was going to blow off.

"Well, it's a good thing you never really got serious with him," Cameron said to Isabelle, sounding like the concerned friend she wasn't.

"Oh, I know!" Isabelle gushed. She gave Liz a condescending smile, then looked back at Cameron. "Then, he's never *really* been good enough for me."

"Then why were you always throwing yourself at him?" Jane asked Isabelle. "Or were you just using him as practice for all the other Dudley boys you've been doing?"

Isabelle's cherubic face turned bright red. Her free-and-easy ways with the prep school set were well known, just like Cameron's wild antics.

Liz smiled down at her tray, sending Jane a silent thank-you.

Cameron ignored Jane and instead went back to addressing Liz. "Look at the bright side, Liz. If Parker *has* lost all his money, you two will have even *more* in common."

Now Liz looked up. "The only new thing we have in common, Cameron, is hating you." Liz got up and stormed out of the cafeteria.

She burst through the doors of the cafeteria, fighting back tears. She strode quickly down the hallway, wanting to put as much distance between herself and Cameron as possible.

"Liz!" Jane called.

Liz stopped and waited for Jane to catch up with her.

"Well, that was brutal," Jane said.

"No kidding," Liz said shakily. "And it's only going to get worse."

Jane tossed her head back to get her thick, long bangs out of her face. "It is all over the papers," she agreed. "And not just the tabloids."

Liz nodded miserably.

"How's Parker holding up?" Jane asked.

Liz fought down the lump in her throat. "I don't know," she admitted hoarsely. "He hasn't returned any of my calls. Or my pages. Or my e-mails. Or anything." She stared down at her boots. "He's totally MIA."

Jane tried to cover her surprise, but not before Liz saw it. "Th-that's bad, huh?" Liz asked.

Jane composed herself and shook her head. "Don't go there," she said. She thought for a minute. "Look, things must be totally out of control at his place. He's probably just unplugged to get a break."

Liz nodded. "Makes sense, I guess. But Jane, wouldn't he want to talk to me? I mean, I'm his girlfriend. If *my* family were falling apart, I'd be calling him every five minutes."

"He's a guy," Jane reminded her. "Guys are weird. You just can't predict them."

"Don't I know it," Liz murmured.

CHAPTER THIRTEEN

don't do anything
I wouldn't do

"It's just so awful about Parker," Lily said. She shoved her calc textbook into her overcrowded locker.

"I know." Adrienne clicked her lock shut. "Liz is totally wrecked."

"Do you think it's true?" Tamara asked, slipping her backpack onto one shoulder.

"I don't know," Adrienne admitted. "I hope not. But Graydon said it's possible. He told me last night that there have been rumors for a while."

"Well, if anyone would know, it would be Graydon," Tamara commented. "His dad and Parker's dad orbit around the same sun."

"Graydon said Devlin stocks did a total nosedive, and a *lot* of their friends lost money," Adrienne said.

"That's got to make it tough for the Devlins to go to

the openings and parties and stuff," Lily said. "Everyone's going to be so mad."

Adrienne nodded. "Graydon says—"

Tamara cut her off with a laugh. "Listen to you! 'Graydon says this' and 'Graydon says that.'"

Adrienne blushed. "Am I that bad?"

"It's cute," Lily said.

"In a dopey, over-the-moon kind of way," Tamara teased. "I still think it's weird that Graydon has done such a personality hundred and eighty."

"Believe me," Adrienne said, "no one is more shocked than I am. But he's been awesome."

"He's certainly showing you a grand ol' time," Tamara said.

"It's not about that," Adrienne protested. "Graydon is actually really sweet."

"Graydon?" a voice repeated behind Adrienne. She turned and saw Brian.

"Did I hear you describe Graydon Warner as 'sweet'?" Brian asked.

"Actually, yes," Adrienne replied.

"So it's true," Brian said. "You're going out with him."

News sure gets around, Adrienne thought. Then she remembered the crowd of kids swarming around the Rolls a few days ago. *We're not exactly keeping a low profile. Brian was bound to find out.*

"Yes, Brian," Adrienne said. "It's true."

Brian shook his head. "Why would you spend even a minute with that snake?"

Adrienne's jaw tensed. "You know, Brian, I don't think it's really any of your business. And you don't know him like I do."

"Come on, Adrienne," Brian scoffed. "Are you really that dumb?"

Lily gasped, and Adrienne's eyes narrowed. "I was smart enough to wise up to you," she retorted. She hated that he could still get to her like this.

Brian took a step backward, stung. He quickly recovered. "Okay, I guess that was harsh."

"You guess?" Adrienne spun her lock and turned to leave. Brian grabbed her elbow to stop her. Adrienne stared at his hand, then up at his face, and he released her.

"I thought we were going to stay friends," he said. "I—I still care about you, you know."

Adrienne sighed. She and Brian had been together for two years, and she had been devastated when he'd dumped her for Cameron. It had taken a lot of hard work to get over him. She didn't want them to be enemies, but she didn't feel all that friendly toward him, either. Certainly not when he was standing there bad-mouthing Graydon.

"You weren't exactly my friend when you hooked up with Cameron, were you?" Adrienne said.

"How many times do I have to say I'm sorry to you?" Brian asked, exasperated.

"You don't. It's over between us, remember? You don't have to do a damn thing," Adrienne said.

"Hey, I wanted to try again," Brian reminded her.

"Is that what this is really about, Brian?" Adrienne asked, a lightbulb going on in her head. "That's it! You are jealous of me and Graydon."

"Please." Brian sneered. "Jealous? Of that lowlife?"

"You sound pretty jealous to me," Adrienne said.

"Me, too," added Lily.

"Me three," Tamara said.

Brian shook his head. "Whatever," he said. "Just don't come crying to me when it all blows up in your face."

"Don't worry," Adrienne retorted, "I won't have to. Come on," she said to Lily and Tamara, "let's get going. This conversation is so over."

"Emma, put down your evidence notebook and start on your piano," Adrienne said. This was the third time Adrienne had given the same instruction. "You are getting behind schedule."

Adrienne had managed to tear Emma away from watching repeats of *CSI* in the kitchen and gotten her to do her homework—despite how many times Emma got distracted by some piece of surveillance equipment in her room. Finally Adrienne dragged the little girl into the living room, where she hoped being away from both TV and high-tech toys would help Emma's concentration.

"Subject seems obsessed with schedules and rules," Emma murmured as she wrote in her notebook. She glanced up and studied Adrienne. She started writing again. "Subject does something funny with her lips when she gets annoyed."

"Okay, Emma, that's it." Adrienne yanked the notebook out from under Emma.

"Hey!" Emma yelped, pencil still held in the air as if she were about to take a note.

"Piano. Now. It's almost dinnertime."

"Fine," Emma grumbled. She slumped her way to the piano and hit a loud chord. "This is all going in the report."

"Maybe I'm keeping my own reports," Adrienne teased.

Emma stared at Adrienne, horrified. Then she frowned. "You wouldn't know how to collect evidence properly. Your reports would be thrown out as inadmissible."

"Bach." Adrienne pointed at the piano. "Begin."

Emma faced the keys and hit the opening notes of the fugue. Adrienne breathed a sigh of relief. Emma's *CSI* obsession was a lot harder to deal with than her previous bout of Oprah-worship.

Now for some of my own homework, Adrienne thought. She settled onto the sofa and pulled open a book.

The room went dark as a pair of strong hands covered her eyes.

"Guess who?" a deep voice asked.

Adrienne smiled. "I think I need more of a hint than that."

She felt warm lips brush her cheek, making her tingle.

"Uhhhhm, Brad Pitt?" she teased.

"Oh, someone much better looking," Graydon joked, releasing her. "Wouldn't you say?"

Adrienne laughed. "You'll do."

He slid onto the sofa with her and kissed her.

"Gross!" Emma exclaimed. "Do you *have* to do that?"

"If you keep practicing like you're supposed to," Adrienne said, "you won't even notice us."

"I'm going to grab a soda," Graydon said, standing up. "Want anything?"

"To be an only child," Emma said.

Graydon laughed and walked out of the room.

Emma spun around on the shiny piano bench. "Break up with him," she told Adrienne.

Surprised, Adrienne stared at Emma. "Why would you say that?"

"Because he's not good for you," Emma said.

Adrienne smiled. Was today declared Jealousy Day or

something? First Brian, and now this? Emma had been bothered when Adrienne had spent time with Cameron, back when Adrienne believed Cameron was actually decent.

She crossed the plush rug and sat beside Emma on the piano bench. "You're awfully nice to worry," she said. "And just because I like Graydon doesn't mean I don't like you."

"I know *that*," Emma said. "I'm not a *child*."

"Actually, Em, you *are*," Adrienne said. "But we'll just keep that our secret."

Emma scowled. "You never listen to me," she said, "and I always end up being right."

Graydon walked back in with his soda and smiled at Emma. She stuck out her tongue at him, then went back to playing the Bach fugue.

"So," Graydon said, "want to grab a drink or some food?"

"I can't," Adrienne said. "I can't leave Emma."

"It's six," Graydon pointed out. "Aren't you supposed to be off now?"

Adrienne glanced at her watch. "True. Let me check with Tania," Adrienne said.

"Does that mean I can stop playing?" Emma asked.

"Looks that way," Adrienne said.

"Yay!" Emma popped off the piano bench.

"Meet you in the hallway," Graydon said.

Adrienne walked Emma into the kitchen, where Tania

was getting dinner ready. She smiled, revealing her gold tooth, when she saw them.

"You have the timing of the perfect," Tania said. "I just ready to come to call you." Then her eyes narrowed and she looked at Emma suspiciously. "Or you know that because of secret spy tool?"

Adrienne laughed. "Don't worry," she said. "I was just coming in to see if it was all right to leave. Emma had nothing to do with it."

"Okay, then." Tania nodded. "Good goings!"

"Good goings to you, too." Adrienne grabbed her stuff and met Graydon in the hallway. He smiled warmly at her, and her knees felt a bit wobbly. *How does he do that?* she wondered with pleasure. *But I hope I do it to him, too.*

"Well, well!" Cameron came around a corner dressed in extremely low-rise jeans and a miniature cashmere sweater barely coming down to her ribs. "Where are you two going?"

"The Carlyle," Graydon said, mentioning the luxury hotel a few blocks north on Madison Avenue.

"Ooh-la-la!" Cameron teased. "Taking a room, Gray?"

"Shut up, Cam," Graydon said, annoyed. "We're going for cocktails." He hit the elevator button again.

"Sure you are, brother dear," Cameron said. "Well, don't do anything I wouldn't do."

"That leaves a lot of room, doesn't it?" Graydon said.

"Hah-hah." Cameron glared at him. "So not funny."

"We're out of here." The elevator door opened, and he and Adrienne stepped inside.

Immediately, Graydon grabbed Adrienne and kissed her passionately. Adrienne pressed her body into his. By the time they arrived at the ground floor, she could barely breathe.

CHAPTER FOURTEEN

---

charge it

"So you want to check out Hush?" Parker asked Liz. "It's supposed to be super hot. We could go tonight, if you're free."

Liz pulled her phone away from her ear and stared at it.

It had been a whole week since she had heard from him. And now he was asking her out on a date, as if everything were totally normal.

"Liz?" his voice came from the phone.

She quickly brought it back to her mouth. "Yeah, sure," she said as casually as possible.

"Great. See you at seven." He clicked off.

Maybe that's how he needs to cope, she thought. *By pretending as if everything is still the same.* Liz was determined that she'd be there for Parker, no matter what it was he needed.

She dialed Adrienne. "Hey, it's me. Listen, I know we were supposed to hang tonight, but Parker just called and asked me to go out."

"That's great!" Adrienne said.

"You're not mad?" Liz asked. "You're cool with it if I ditch you?"

"Of course!" Adrienne assured her. "Parker has finally come around. You've been going crazy not hearing from him."

"True," Liz admitted.

"Hey, why don't you still sleep over? You already set it up with your mom. And we can go over every detail of your fabulous date with Parker."

"Great idea. See you tonight."

An hour later, Liz hopped into a cab and sailed downtown. Hush was a new hot spot in the meatpacking district, a neighborhood that was once gritty and scary but was now filled with cutting-edge designers' stores and celebrity hangouts.

Liz paid for the cab and got out, running lightly across the cobblestones in her high heels. Tall, thin women and expensively dressed men climbed out of limos or strolled the crooked streets and window-shopped around her. Paparazzi snapped pix of the young stars of a hot WB teen-soap walking into the restaurant ahead of her.

Parker was right, Liz thought as the sleekly dressed doorman held open the door for her, *this place is seriously happening.*

"Welcome to Hush," the hostess greeted her. The

young woman was as beautiful as any of the celebrities in the place. Liz figured that being hot must be a job requirement, since every single person working there—from the waitresses to the busboys to the bartenders—was drop-dead gorgeous.

"I'm meeting Parker Devlin," Liz said.

The woman gave her a startled look but recovered quickly. "Do you have a reservation?" she asked, glancing down at the thick book on the hostess stand.

"I—I think so," Liz said. She realized that the hostess must have heard the news. *I suppose all of New York City knows the Devlin name now—and not just for the records and movies they've produced.*

"Ah, yes, here it is." The hostess smiled graciously at Liz, obviously wanting to make up for her almost faux pas. "Mr. Devlin hasn't arrived yet. Would you like to wait in the lounge or at the table?"

"The table, please," Liz said, beginning to feel a little self-conscious standing alone and surrounded by so many beautiful people.

"And may I check your coat?" the hostess offered.

"Thanks," Liz said, handing over her heavy winter coat.

The hostess nodded to a handsome young man in a severe black jacket and baggy black pants. He strode over to the hostess stand. "Giancarlo will see you to your table," the hostess said.

"This way, please," Giancarlo said in a melodic Italian accent.

Liz followed him through the candlelit restaurant. The bar area was set up as a lounge, with cozy love seats and overstuffed chairs and small tables scattered around. Giancarlo led her past a wide staircase leading downstairs.

"What's down there?" Liz asked.

"The dance floor," Giancarlo explained. "And another bar. Here we are."

He placed two menus on a table near a window in the dining area. In the center of the table was a small bowl of water with a flower floating in it. Liz sat down and admired the soft lighting, the jewellike tones of the tablecloth and napkins, and the luxurious leather of the seats. The effect was rich but not pretentious, fancy but fun.

"This place is beautiful," Liz murmured.

"That's why you fit in so well," Parker said, arriving at the table. He turned to Giancarlo. "Can you bring us a couple of mango-tinis?"

"Of course." Giancarlo vanished into the cavernous space.

Parker gave Liz a quick kiss and then dropped into the seat opposite her. He seemed a bit distracted. Liz wondered if maybe he was high.

"So, Gorgeous," he said. "What do you think of the joint?"

"It's fantastic, of course. But—"

"Only the best, right?"

There was an edge to Parker's voice that was new. He wasn't high, Liz realized. He was totally stressed. Liz was certain he'd feel better if he opened up to her.

"Parker," she said softly, "what is going on?"

A cloud passed across his face. He drummed his fingers on the table. Giancarlo reappeared with the drinks. Liz waited patiently for the waiter to set their glasses down and leave them alone—she was pretty certain Parker was not going to confide in her with anyone in earshot.

"Parker?" Liz pressed.

"You sure you want to hear this?" he asked.

Liz nodded.

He took a sip of his mango-flavored drink. "Just remember—you asked. Okay. Let's see. Where do I begin? It's all such a mess."

"Was this a huge shock to you?" Liz asked.

"Things have been weird for a while," Parker admitted. "My dad was always a workaholic, but he went into overdrive about two months ago. He even started bringing work home." Parker gave a sharp bitter laugh. "Well, at first I thought it was work. Mostly it was stuff he was shredding. I asked him what was going on, and at first he wouldn't tell me. Finally, he confessed that he was in big trouble." Parker looked at her sadly. "He wanted me to help him figure out how to break it to my mom."

"And did you?" Liz asked.

Parker shook his head. "I just told him to tell her before she heard about it on the news. The way everyone else did. The way the entire world did."

Liz reached for his hand, but he picked up his glass instead.

"Mom *freaked*. She started screaming that she had always known he was a crook, and that he had disgraced the family, and that she never should have married him because he was such a social step down."

"She said that?" Liz said with horror. She couldn't imagine her mother saying something so cruel to her about her dad. Even when her parents were going through their divorce, neither of them had said anything negative about the other in front of her.

"Yup, she said that," Parker said. He held up his glass again and clinked Liz's. "To Devlin family values."

"I'm so sorry," Liz said. "So that explains the phone calls and the weird behavior."

"Pretty much." Parker nodded. "That was Dad keeping me posted on what was happening with all of the subpoenas and meetings and stuff."

"So now what happens?" Liz asked.

"Well, unless Dad's lawyers can work out a legal miracle, the Devlins and our so-called 'media empire' are through."

"Everything will be fine," Liz assured him. As soon as the words were out of her mouth, she realized how lame she sounded. Parker's expression confirmed it.

"How can you possibly say that?" he demanded, his voice incredulous. "Trust me, Liz, as this case gets more publicity—and believe me, it will—everyone in New York will cut me and my family off. I've seen it happen to other families."

"It won't happen with me, Parker," Liz said. "I never cared about the money. I care about you."

"You know what?" Parker said. "Let's stop talking about this. Let's just have a nice time, eat a great dinner, have some fantastic desserts, and then do some serious dancing downstairs."

Liz forced herself to smile. "Works for me," she said lightly. But she could tell something had changed. She only hoped it wasn't their whole relationship.

"Great tunes," Parker shouted into Liz's ear.

Liz nodded; she knew there was no point in trying to be heard over the loud sound system. They had finished dinner and were dancing in the downstairs lounge.

Parker pulled Liz into him and kissed her. "Ready to go?"

Liz nodded. By the time they had gotten their entrées, the tension between them had lifted. Liz felt as if they were finally back on track. Parker took her hand and led her up to their table again.

Giancarlo instantly reappeared. "Anything else?" he asked.

"No thanks," Parker said, "just the bill, please."

"Now," Liz said, reaching for her purse, "I insist, we are splitting this."

Parker smiled. "You're sweet," he said, "but no. I'm not that broke yet."

The check came, and Parker didn't even look at it—he just threw his black American Express Card on it. The first time Liz saw the card she hadn't even been sure what it was—it looked so weird. That's when Parker explained that the black "Centurion" Card was only for people who spent more than $100,000 a month. Parker had had one since he was twelve, courtesy of his father.

They smiled at each other as they waited for Giancarlo to come back. Liz was already anticipating being alone with Parker in the town car. From the way he was looking at her, she had a feeling he was looking forward to the same thing.

Giancarlo returned and leaned close to Parker. Liz could barely hear him as he said, "Sir, would you like to try another card?"

"Is there a problem?" Parker asked.

"I'd suggest trying another one," Giancarlo said.

Parker shrugged. "Okay," he said. "Just bring back the other one."

"Sir," Giancarlo whispered, "I'm afraid American Express asked me to keep it. I would lose my job if I returned it. Would you like to try another card?"

Liz looked at Parker. She suddenly knew that he didn't have another card. He had never needed one other than the black AmEx.

"I'll handle this," Liz said. "Do you take cash?"

"More than pleased to," Giancarlo said, obviously relieved that there would be no scene.

"Liz, you can't," Parker said, his face reddening.

"I can, and I will," Liz said, taking the check. She opened it up and glanced at it.

Liz blinked, staring at the shockingly high number. With tip, she'd have about twenty dollars left for the rest of the weekend, and no more cash until she got paid next week. And there went the two hundred dollars a week she was supposed to be putting aside for college. Liz swallowed, then placed the money in the folder.

"Any change?" the waiter asked.

"No, that's fine," Liz said.

"Thank you," Giancarlo said, and zoomed off.

Parker rose without a word and moved quickly out of the restaurant, not even glancing back at Liz.

Liz followed him, then realized the hostess had taken

her coat. She redeemed the coat check ticket, plunking down five, then raced out into the street. Parker was walking east and didn't even seem to care that he'd left her behind.

"Parker!" she called. "Parker, wait a sec."

He spun around and she ran to catch up with him. "What?" he demanded. "Are you happy? Did you have a nice time watching me get humiliated in there?"

Liz was aghast. "What are you talking about?" she asked, completely perplexed. "When the card got rejected, I didn't see the problem in paying. You've paid so much for me. It's no big deal."

"It *is* a big deal!" Parker shouted. "In all my life, I've never been so embarrassed. I couldn't pay the check, and so a *nanny* lays out her *babysitting* money to cover my meal? Do you realize how *twisted* that is?"

Liz stepped back as if she had been struck. *How can he be saying this to me?*

"I just can't do this," Parker said. "This is just way too hard. Until this is all straightened out, I just can't—" He shook his head. "I'm done."

Parker spun around and ran across Greenwich Street, leaving Liz behind on the sidewalk, stunned.

CHAPTER FIFTEEN

unsteady gait

Liz stood leaning against the wall of the Claremont Riding Academy, her eyes half closed. After her miserable evening with Parker, she had gone to Adrienne's as planned. She and Adrienne had rehashed the scene over and over, examining every detail, every word he'd said. But even though Adrienne was her best friend, she couldn't fix the hurt Parker had caused. After Adrienne had finally conked out, Liz cried herself to sleep.

Now, at quarter past eight in the morning, Liz stared gloomily into the tiny Claremont riding ring. Luckily, David was spending the day with a socially acceptable play-mate, so she only had Heather to worry about.

I really should have refused this extra workday, Liz thought, although after last night, the additional money would help make up for the money she'd spent on dinner instead of her college fund.

Heather, saddled up on Mindreader's back, clung to

the reins with her face frozen in the mingled expression of terror and misery that had become her trademark.

"Heather!" Alexandra Winters shouted. "You look like a rag doll out there! Post, child! Post!"

Heather attempted to lift herself in the saddle, but with each attempt, she smashed back into the rising saddle of the trotting horse.

"You have an unsteady gait! Stop!" Ms. Winters moved into the ring and, with one sharp look at Mindreader, she stopped the horse in its tracks. She walked over and grabbed the horse's bridle so she could talk to Heather.

"Can't you feel the horse's rhythm?" she asked.

"All I feel is sick," Heather whined.

"Come on, Heather, I know that you can do this."

"Every time I go down, she goes up," Heather complained.

"Watch her right front leg," Ms. Winters instructed. "When her right front leg goes forward, she'll be coming up. What does that mean?"

"When her leg goes forward, I go up?" Heather asked.

"If you're going counterclockwise in a ring, yes. Just pay attention to the rise and fall of her haunch. Now try again."

Heather sighed, and Mindreader slowly moved into a trot. As Liz watched, Heather's petrified expression gave way to astonishment as she began to rise and fall correctly.

Mindreader snorted approvingly. It was obvious that she had hated Heather smashing onto her back as much as Heather had.

"Good girl, Heather!" Ms. Winters shouted. "Can you feel the rhythm?"

"Yes!" Heather shouted.

"Okay," Ms. Winters shouted. "Now keep posting while I have the horse change direction!"

Liz held her breath—she really hoped Heather was up to the task.

Ms. Winters tugged Mindreader's lead line, and the horse did a figure eight in the ring, switching directions. As the gait changed, Heather changed with it in a seamless post.

Liz was astonished. Heather actually looked like a pro. "Awesome, Heather!" she shouted.

"I'm doing it!" Heather screeched. "Look at me! I'm doing it!"

"Goooooo, Heather!" Liz cheered. She pumped her arms in the air. "Wooo-hoo!" She had never seen Heather look so proud of herself. It was great to see. Even the stoic, businesslike Ms. Winters looked ecstatic.

"You have it, all right," Ms. Winters shouted. "You'll never forget it—it's like riding a bike."

"I can't ride a bike," Heather said.

"Well, it looks like you're starting to be able to ride a

horse," Ms. Winters declared with a smile. She signaled Mindreader to stop. Heather sat astride the horse, beaming.

"You've made great progress. Let's call it quits for the day."

"Absolutely not!" Dr. M–C screeched from the doorway. "Heather, stay on that horse!"

Liz watched as Dr. M–C crossed the ring, carefully avoiding the piles left by Mindreader during her morning exercise.

"Alex-AHN-dra!" she drawled. "Look!" She thrust a paper at the instructor.

Ms. Winters took it and scanned it. "You're not serious," she said in a flat voice.

"Deadly."

Uh-oh, Liz thought. She'd heard that tone in Dr. M–C's voice before. Whether Ms. Winters knew it or not, Liz was certain Dr. M–C was going to get her way. She wondered what exactly was on that piece of paper.

"Dr. Markham-Collins," Ms. Winters said, her own voice steely. "The Knickerbocker Junior Equestrian Competition is serious business. Heather simply isn't ready to compete."

"She's only registered for level-one walk-trot," Dr. M–C protested. "That's for beginners."

"Heather posted for the first time *today*," Ms. Winters said. "She has no ring training, and she cannot anticipate the movements of the animal. She has no—"

"She has *you*," Dr. M-C interrupted. "You said you trained champions!"

"I do!" Ms. Winters declared, obviously insulted that her credentials were being questioned. "But the Knicker-bocker? In three weeks?"

"It would be your greatest achievement!" Dr. M-C cajoled. "I'd tell everyone you were responsible. Everyone."

"Well . . ." Ms. Winters looked at Heather, whose expression had returned to terror/misery mode.

Please don't give in, Liz silently begged. She had a feeling Heather was wishing the exact same thing.

"Well, I guess we could *try*," Ms. Winters concluded. "But I warn you, I will not send that child into the ring unless she is completely prepared."

"As I am sure she will be!" declared Dr. M-C triumphantly.

"She'll have to come every single day," Ms. Winters said.

Liz sighed. *Which means I'll be here every day, too.* Although, with the way things were going with Parker, maybe she could use the distraction.

Suddenly, Dr. M-C's cell phone rang out loudly from her bag.

The horse whinnied and shied, moving sideways. Heather clung to the reins and let out a shriek. "Help me!"

Ms. Winters lunged for the line but missed. "Pull back

on the reins and squeeze your legs, Heather!" she shouted.

Heather stayed glued to the saddle, leaning forward and pulling back on the reins. Slowly, Mindreader came to a halt. Dr. M-C rummaged through her oversized bag for her phone the entire time.

Whoa, Liz thought, impressed by Heather's surprising ability to follow Ms. Winters's orders without letting a panic attack completely overwhelm her.

"Am I—am I okay?" Heather asked shakily.

"You're awesome!" Liz shouted to her.

"Great handling, Heather!" Ms. Winters called to her. "You'll be a horsewoman yet!"

"I told you!" Dr. M-C said, unconcerned. "Hello?" she said, finally answering her phone. "Oh, hel-LO, Binky! No, I'm just at Heather's riding lesson. She just pulled a crazed horse back into line. She has all the makings of a horse-woman, Alex-AHN-dra says. Really? Darien, too? Which division, darling? NO! What fun! We'll have to sit together and root for our girls! Kiss, kiss."

Dr. M-C shut her phone and turned to Liz, Heather, and Ms. Winters, fuming.

"Can you imagine the gall?" she asked incredulously, "Binky Darrel has enrolled her daughter in the Knickerbocker level-one division. Can you imagine putting that kind of pressure on a child?"

"Can I come down now?" Heather asked in a small

voice. Liz could tell the little girl was still shaken by her experience.

"Of course," Ms. Winters said, grabbing the reins and helping her dismount.

"Thank you, Alex-AHN-dra. You'll whip Heather into shape, I'm sure."

"Heather," Liz said to the little girl as she approached her on shaky knees. "I was so proud of the way you handled yourself when Mindreader spooked. You were great."

"It was scary," Heather said.

"But you handled it," Liz said. "Even though you were afraid, you did exactly the right thing. You didn't let the feeling of being scared take you over."

Heather thought a moment. "I knew that Mindreader didn't *want* to hurt me. She was just scared of the noise. I just had to calm her down."

Liz stared at Heather as an amazing thought filled her mind. *It's the same with Parker,* she realized. *He's just scared of the noise that other people are making about his father's problems. I need to make him realize that none of this nonsense has to do with how we feel about each other.*

Wow. I just got a life lesson from Heather! Liz dropped to her knees and gave the extremely surprised girl a bone-crushing bear hug.

"Are you all right?" Heather asked.

"I will be." Liz grinned.

CHAPTER SIXTEEN

making plans

"Liz was totally wrecked when she slept over," Adrienne said to Graydon. Adrienne and Graydon were finishing their Sunday brunch at Paola's, a funky little bistro on the Upper East Side. "She's really torn up about Parker. I don't get it. Why would he want to break up with her now?"

"She should consider herself lucky," Graydon said. "I hate to say it, but the Devlins are ruined. And it's only going to get worse." He shrugged. "Parker just recognized the inevitable and did Liz a favor. At least now she doesn't have the guilt of breaking up with *him*." He took a sip of his latte.

Adrienne gaped at him. "That's a terrible thing to say," she said. "If your dad was involved in some kind of scandal, I wouldn't dump *you*. Would you dump me if the situation was reversed?"

Graydon laughed. "Adrienne, I can't even *imagine* your parents doing anything that would cause a scandal. That hypothetical is so out of the realm of reality, I can't even consider it."

"But, still—" Adrienne pressed.

"Look, Adrienne," Graydon said. "I'm sorry your friend is caught up in Parker's mess. I'm only saying that distancing herself from it isn't such a bad idea. Besides, Parker is going to seriously need some space to deal with all that's going on. Having to worry about a girlfriend, too, might push him right over the edge."

"I guess . . ." Adrienne picked up her orange juice.

Graydon reached across the table and took Adrienne's other hand. "I know you're upset about your friend," he said, "and that's one of the things I love about you."

Adrienne flushed with pleasure. Graydon had never used the word "love" with her before.

"But let's change the subject to something more pleasant," he said. "It's my mission to keep you happy, remember?"

"I think you may have mentioned that in the past." Adrienne smiled.

"So now you can make *me* happy," Graydon said, leaning toward her over the table.

"How?" Adrienne asked. A nervous thrill went through her. *Is he going to suggest what I think he is about to suggest?* she wondered. *Is he going to ask me if I'm ready to sleep with him?*

To her total astonishment, she realized her answer would be yes! How amazing—and terrifying was that?

"You seem a million miles away, all of a sudden," Graydon said. "Did you hear my question?"

Adrienne blushed and stared down at her plate. She was so wrapped up in thinking about having her first time with him that she had totally tuned him out! "Sorry. So what were you saying?

"You *were* totally on another planet, weren't you?" Graydon laughed. "What were you thinking about?"

"Nothing," Adrienne insisted. "Seriously!" She was NOT going to tell him what she had actually been thinking! "Now please tell me what you asked me while I was visiting Mars!"

Graydon leaned back in his chair and smiled a slow, lazy smiled. He took a long sip of his Bloody Mary.

"Graydon!" Adrienne pressed, giggling. "*Tell* me."

"Okay, I'll stop torturing you. I just invited you to the Young Lions Benefit next weekend. As my date. I mean—" He cleared his throat and sat up straight. "*I mean*—" he said in a totally fake pretentious voice, "as the date of the co-chair of the hottest social event of the season."

Adrienne's green eyes widened. "Really?"

Graydon nodded. "Really!"

"I would love to go with you! Thank you!" Then she frowned.

"What's wrong?" Graydon asked.

"I have absolutely nothing to wear!" Adrienne wailed.

Graydon shook his head, amused. He flipped open his cell phone. "You girls. So predictable." He hit speed-dial. "Cam?" he said into the phone, his warm, dark eyes never leaving Adrienne's face. "I have a favor to ask you. . . ."

Four hours later, Adrienne was in the Warners' Rolls-Royce beside Cameron. They had just finished a fitting at the studio of some designer friend of Cameron's and now they were off to buy shoes.

Adrienne's head was spinning. What was she doing out on a shopping spree with Cam? *Could the fact that Graydon really likes me actually be getting Cameron to treat me with a smidge of decency?*

Nah.

Adrienne figured Cam was just humoring Graydon so that in the future she could claim that he owed her. Besides, Cameron never turned down an opportunity to go shopping.

Might as well enjoy it while I can. Shopping with Cameron definitely came with perks: the best treatment, the best clothes, and the highest price tags.

The car pulled up in front of Manolo Blahnik's tiny boutique on West Fifty-fourth Street, near the Museum of Modern Art.

The girls walked into the atelier, where shoes were displayed like works of art, on tables, hanging on the walls, and in Lucite boxes.

"Cameron!" one of the salesgirls greeted them. "Welcome back!"

"Hey, Maria," Cameron said. "Special request."

Adrienne looked around at the store. Liz was a shoe freak, but Adrienne didn't quite get them. Sure, they made her legs looks great, but *hours* on them made her crazy. She was more of a casual gal—sandals and low mules were more her style.

"Anything for the Warners," Maria chirped. "What do we need today?"

As Cameron and Maria discussed possibilities, Adrienne's eyes wandered. Through the window, she saw a confused-looking floral delivery guy carrying a big bouquet of roses. He peered through the glass, and entered.

"Miss Lewis?" he asked.

"Here!" Adrienne called, raising her hand.

"For you," he said. "Sign."

They must be from Graydon, she realized. Who else knew she would be here?

Adrienne signed the slip and handed the delivery guy a tip.

"I'm supposed to wait for an answer," the guy said.

"Oh?" Adrienne quickly opened the card.

"I'm at a party at the St. Regis," the card said. "If you want to come and rescue me from terminal boredness, send one rose back. If you don't, send them all. Gray."

Adrienne blushed beet red, pulled a rose from the bouquet, and handed it back to the delivery guy, who winked.

Graydon is just too adorable for words, Adrienne thought. *And he is seriously nuts about me.*

CHAPTER SEVENTEEN

the scam

"I want a balloon," David demanded Friday afternoon. He tugged Liz's jeans and pointed back toward the entrance of the Central Park Zoo.

It had been more than a week since Liz's awful dinner at Hush and Adrienne's shopping spree with Cameron. For the first time, Adrienne felt awkward with her best friend—she felt guilty that her romance with Graydon was heating up so spectacularly while Liz's with Parker was falling apart. She really wanted to be there for Liz, so she had suggested they take advantage of the springlike March weather and get together in spite of their nanny duties.

"I promise I'll buy you a balloon later, David," Liz said. "But right now you kids are going to look at the animals, and Adrienne and I are going to talk."

"If we had stayed at the apartment, you could have talked there and I wouldn't have to wander around here with these *children*." Emma crossed her arms over her chest.

Heather whipped around to face Emma. "I'm older than *you!*" she snapped at Emma.

"Not mentally," Emma countered.

"*I* can control an animal that outweighs me by several tons," Heather said haughtily. "So watch it. I can use a crop on you, too."

Emma stared at Heather. Adrienne stared, too—she'd never seen the girl so assertive with Emma before. *Way to go, Heather,* she thought.

"Let's get them to the seals," Adrienne suggested. "The show starts in a minute, and even Emma becomes engrossed. We can talk while they watch."

"Sounds good to me," Liz said.

"I *hate* the seals!" Emma protested. "*CSI* is on!"

"Seals, or no TV ever," Adrienne threatened.

"You can't do that," Emma said. "You *know* that I need to see *CSI!*"

"Watch me," Adrienne warned. "I can screw up the controls of a satellite-fed plasma TV so thoroughly, you will never get it to work again."

"You *can't*," Emma whined.

"Try me," Adrienne said. "Easy choice: the seals, or no TV till puberty."

Emma's eyes widened in horror, then her mouth twisted into an odd smile. "Okay," she said, apparently giving in. "As long as we go to the snake house next."

"Thank you, Emma," Adrienne said. "I would *love* to see the snakes with you."

"Oh," Emma replied, obviously disappointed that the idea of snakes didn't freak out Adrienne.

"So seals it is," Adrienne said.

"Hey, Heather, race you!" David said. He dashed toward the seal pool, darting through the strolling families. Heather galloped behind him on an invisible horse. Emma glared at Adrienne, then slowly followed the other two.

"I have a feeling I'll pay for that later," Adrienne said. "Now tell me what's going on with you."

Liz looked at the three kids crowding around the seal pool with scores of other children and their parents. She shook her head. "I don't even know anymore," she said. "I'm just so confused."

"Still no word from Parker?" Adrienne asked.

Liz shook her head. "And I feel like after the way he just stalked away from me last weekend, he should be the one trying to get in touch with *me*."

"Have you called him?" Adrienne asked.

Liz stared down at her shoes. "Yes," she said. "I left a message on his voice mail saying we needed to talk. He ignored it." She ran her hands through her curls. Adrienne noticed Liz had dark circles under her eyes.

"Ever since Parker and I started going out I've been kind of preparing for when he dumped me," Liz admitted.

"That doesn't sound like much fun," Adrienne said.

Liz shrugged. "I thought I was being realistic, you know? I figured he'd find some Park Avenue heiress, and that would be it."

"If he wanted a Park Avenue heiress," Adrienne pointed out, "he'd have gotten one. He's dated them before. He likes *you.*"

Liz swallowed hard. "I thought maybe he was just, I don't know, going out with me because I was different. Exotic. The scholarship girl."

"But you know now that's not true," Adrienne said.

"But that's what makes it so hard!" Liz exclaimed, her voice breaking. "I could have handled him going after some-one more in his crowd. More like what he's used to. Instead, he's breaking up with me because he's going through a bad time and he doesn't want to share it with me." She took in a deep breath. "He doesn't trust me with the serious stuff."

Adrienne thought for a moment. "Maybe that's not really it. Maybe he wants to *protect* you."

Liz looked at Adrienne, and Adrienne could see that her eyes were shiny from the tears she was fighting to hold back. "Wh-what do you mean?"

"Graydon said that it's only going to get worse for the Devlins. There's going to be a lot of gossip, and a lot of media attention. Some of that attention could wind up on you. Parker probably wouldn't want that to happen.

Besides, with everything that's going on with his family, dating and romance are not exactly a priority."

Liz nodded very slowly. "Jane said something kind of similar. Girls want to confide in their best friends, but guys don't really talk a lot when they're freaking out."

"Exactly," Adrienne said. "Once things calm down, he'll be able to focus again."

"You know what I hate?" Liz said. "All the girls at P-B see that we're on hold. Isabelle Schyler actually came up to me on Friday and congratulated me for dumping him! I look just as shallow as Cam and Mimi and the rest of them. As if I were after his money the whole time, and there was nothing real to our relationship at all."

"Who cares what they think?" Adrienne said. "*You* know that's not true."

"But how do I make *Parker* believe it?" Liz asked.

"They all live in such a weird bubble," Adrienne said. "Their worldview is so skewed, it's hard to get someone like Parker to really understand where you're coming from." She looked at David, Emma, and Heather, completely engaged by the seals. She shook her head. "I think that these kids never just have basic fun. They're being raised to think that it's not a good time unless you end up with a gift bag full of iPods."

Liz nodded. "Or if your birthday party isn't catered and star-studded."

"Or if the underwear for summer camp isn't La Perla."

"Or if you don't go from your riding lesson to the Olympics . . ." Liz trailed off.

"You okay?" Adrienne asked.

"*That's it!*" Liz exclaimed, causing a seal to turn and bark at her. "No wonder Parker is freaking out. He doesn't know how to be a boyfriend without spending big bucks. He's never just gone out and had plain old fun!"

"You may be onto something," Adrienne said.

"He thinks that unless it's a five-hundred-dollar dinner, it's not eating," Liz said. "Or that if the music isn't coming out of the speakers of the hottest club, it's not music. It always has to be a production number for him. And if he can't offer that to a date, what's he got? Who is he? That's what I have to show him—I don't need any of that to have a good time with him."

"Liz, are you sure?" Adrienne asked skeptically. "You and I can lie in Central Park and gab, or grab a slice of pizza at Two Boots in the Village, or go window-shopping and not actually *buy* anything. I don't know if Parker's up for real life, do you?"

Liz smiled. "The great thing about *real* life is that it belongs to *you*. You can make it up as you go along! And if I can get Parker out into it, I can also make him see that none of this stuff happening to his dad has anything to do with *us*."

"I don't know," Adrienne said. "He's pretty down."

"His dad isn't *dying*," Liz said. "So Parker's not as rich as he used to be. Should I like him any less? If the Warners lost all their money, would you abandon Graydon?"

"I don't think it would be an issue," Adrienne said. "It seems like Parker's identity is all wrapped up in being his dad's kid. Graydon's really his own guy. He's like a changeling in that family."

"He *is* cute," Liz admitted.

Adrienne smiled. Now that it seemed as if her friend was feeling a bit stronger, Adrienne felt more comfortable talking about Graydon. She'd been desperate to talk to Liz ever since she had come to the momentous realization that she thought she was ready to go all the way with Graydon. In fact, she was starting to make plans—the night of the benefit would be *the* night. "You know, Liz," she said, blushing a little.

"Yes?" Liz said, turning to her friend.

"About Graydon. Graydon and me. I think I want to . . . I mean, that after the benefit . . ." She stopped.

"Adrienne, no." Liz's eyes widened.

"Yes," Adrienne said, nodding. "I think I'm in love." Just saying the words made her feel flushed and shy. "And . . . and I'm pretty sure Graydon loves me, too. Everything about the way he treats me makes it seem that way. I-I think that I'm ready to go further."

"Are you serious?" Liz said.

"I'm seriously sick." Emma groaned behind them.

Adrienne whirled around to see Emma doubled over and clutching her stomach. "I thought you were watching the seals," she said. *Did she hear our conversation?*

"I was practicing tailing a suspect." Emma moaned. "But now my stomach is killing me!"

Adrienne knelt down beside Emma. "Okay, don't worry. I'll get you right home." She thought maybe Emma was faking it to get away from David and Heather, but she wasn't going to risk it. "Sorry," she told Liz.

"No problem," Liz said. "But we still have to talk about *you!*"

"I'll call you later," Adrienne promised.

"You'd better!" Liz said. "This needs more discussion."

Emma tugged her hand. "Let's go!"

"We're going," Adrienne said.

"I think we'll hang here awhile," Liz said. "The kids are actually having plain old fun for a change."

Adrienne and Emma hurried out of the park and back to 841 Fifth Avenue, Emma moaning the entire way.

As soon as they arrived upstairs, Emma ran to her room. *Is she going to barf?* Adrienne worried, following. But when she entered Emma's bedroom, the little girl was rummaging through piles of CDs on her desk. She seemed to have had a miraculous recovery.

"How's your stomach?" Adrienne narrowed her eyes.

"That was a ruse," Emma said. "A scam. A ploy."

"No kidding." Adrienne shook her head, her frustration growing. "Emma, it is *not*—"

"But it was for your own good!" Emma held up a CD. "You have to listen to this!"

Adrienne looked at Emma's desk. "What are all these CDs?" she asked.

"Data," Emma said. "Conversations. For evidence."

"You've been taping people?" Adrienne's eyes widened. "Emma, I told you that you couldn't secretly record people anymore."

Now Emma's expression grew cagey. "Ohhhhhhh. I thought you meant I couldn't *video*tape anymore. You didn't say anything about audio!"

Adrienne sighed. If there was a loophole, Emma would always find it.

Before Adrienne could figure out how to respond, Emma popped the CD in her stereo and Cameron's voice filled the room.

"She's such a little bitch," Cameron said. "I'd do anything to get rid of her."

"Would you?" Graydon asked. "Really?" Even though it was just his voice, Adrienne grinned. She could hear him smiling.

"She gets under my skin," Cameron complained. "I thought the whole newspaper thing would help, but it didn't."

Cameron is talking about Mimi, Adrienne realized.

"So what do you want *me* to do about it, Cam?" Graydon said. "I'm in *college.* I don't have time for your silly high school games."

"I want you to seduce her and drop her," Cameron wheedled.

"No way!" Graydon said.

Thatta boy! Adrienne was thrilled that Graydon wouldn't do anything so sleazy.

"I want her wrecked," Cameron insisted. "Her reputation, her emotions, her job."

Wait a minute, Adrienne thought. *What job? Mimi doesn't work!*

"Forget it," Graydon said. "I don't want to waste my time on a little nothing like her."

"Well, I guess if you're not up to it . . ." Cameron taunted.

"What do you mean 'not up to it'?" Graydon demanded. "I just don't want to. She's not worth my time."

"Sure, fine, whatever." Now Cameron sounded bored.

"You know I could do it," Graydon pressed.

"Just forget it, Gray."

"I don't want to forget it," Graydon said. "In fact, let's make this interesting. Let's put a little wager on it."

Adrienne's brow furrowed. *Could Graydon actually be*

going along with this horrible plot?

"I know," Cameron said, her voice excited again. "If you do it, if you seduce her and dump her, I'll give you my convertible at the beach."

"Okay," Graydon agreed. "And if I don't manage it—and you *know* that's not going to happen, but in case every law of the universe goes awry, I'll buy you that coat at J. Mendel you keep whining about."

That is so wrong! Adrienne thought. *I can't believe that Graydon could be so . . . so like Cameron!*

"Deal!" Cameron exclaimed. It sounded to Adrienne as if the two schemers had high-fived. "The day she leaves, either you get the keys . . ."

"Or you get the coat."

Cameron giggled. "I guess either way I win. You know," she added thoughtfully. "I almost feel sorry for her."

Me, too! Adrienne thought.

"Why?" Graydon asked.

"Because she'll never know what hit her," Cameron said. "Poor Adrienne."

Poor Adrienne.

Adrienne turned off the CD player, her hand shaking. *They're talking about me!*

CHAPTER EIGHTEEN

free love

"**I** told you Graydon shouldn't be your boyfriend," Emma declared. "*Now* maybe you'll believe me."

Adrienne numbly looked from the CD player to Emma. She was too upset to even speak. Too upset to even cry. All she could do was stare at Emma in shock.

"So don't be all in love with him like you said," Emma said. "He's not good enough for you."

Adrienne smiled in spite of her pain. "You got that right," she said weakly. Emma had heard her conversation with Liz and didn't want Adrienne to make the biggest mistake of her life. Emma actually cared about her. At the moment, that meant the world to her.

"Now maybe you won't be mad that I didn't listen to you, right?" Emma wheedled. "And agree that *CSI* totally rules."

Adrienne took in a shaky breath, trying to stay focused, trying to process this incredible betrayal by

Graydon. "It–it's still wrong that you tape people behind their backs," Adrienne said. Then she squeezed the girl in a tight hug. "But thank you for playing this for me."

"You should hear the other stuff Cameron and Graydon talk about." Emma reached for the player again.

"No," Adrienne said. "I don't want to hear." She didn't think she could take hearing their voices, or anything else they might have said about her.

"Okay," Emma said. "They say mean things about everybody. Mostly about you and Mimi, though."

Adrienne swallowed hard, afraid she was going to be sick. What other horrible things could they have said? *No. Don't torture yourself like this,* she told herself. *Do* not *listen to these tapes.*

Then another nauseating idea occurred to her. What if Emma had played these conversations for anyone else? *I'll be branded as the total loser of the universe,* she thought, her cheeks reddening. *I have to destroy them!*

"Listen, Emma," she said, collecting the CDs, "I'm going to take these."

"But—" Emma began.

Adrienne held up a hand to stop her. "No. I need to take them." She tucked the CDs into her bag, then turned back to Emma. "Since you don't have an actual stomachache, why don't we see if Tania has a snack for you?" She wanted to get out of there as quickly as possible. She wasn't sure how much longer she could keep it together. She figured Tania wouldn't mind if she left early.

In the elevator Adrienne thought she would start sobbing, but she took a deep breath and held it together. When she stepped out into the warm spring evening, she looked up and down Fifth Avenue, relieved Graydon wasn't pulling another one of his surprise grand appearances, and hurried toward the subway.

I really thought he was falling in love with me, she thought, a horrible leaden feeling invading her entire body. *Instead, I was falling right into their game. How could I have been so stupid?*

Adrienne wasn't sure which felt worse: that the guy she thought she loved was a complete skank or that she had been set up and played for a total fool by Cameron.

She's done it to me again, Adrienne thought. *I cannot let her get away with it this time.*

Adrienne went to dump the CDs in a corner garbage can but stopped.

Conversations. She stared at the discs in her hand. *Cameron's private conversations.*

"Cameron had better be prepared for a real shock," she murmured, slipping the CDs back into her bag.

Saturday morning, Heather paced back and forth near the riding rings at Madison Square Garden. She was in her riding clothes: beige jodhpurs, well-tailored jacket, and velvet riding cap. Her wild curls had been tamed by Ms. Winters into two neat braids that hung down her back, the ends carefully wrapped and tied with black silk ribbon. Heather looked bright and alert, but very nervous.

Liz stood at Heather's side, patting her shoulder. She had never been "eventing" (as Ms. Winters called participating in the competition), and she had had no idea what to expect. For the Knickerbocker show there were two rings set up: one with jumps, the other without.

The competitions seemed to run simultaneously. The crowd alternately recognized one rider or the other as they competed in different events, and so just as one rider was performing a difficult jump or move, the audience would cheer for the rider in the other ring. *That would drive me nuts*, Liz thought. *How do those girls stay so focused?*

Liz recognized Mitzi Huntington's daughter, Kelli, in the next ring, looking as if she had ridden every day of her life. Kelli was twelve—three years older than Heather—and already looked like a seasoned pro. She easily cleared the first few low jumps, expertly demonstrating her careful control of the horse. As she neared the final and largest jump, her horse slowed slightly and, instead of sailing over the wide jump, clipped the rail with his rear hoof and knocked it down.

"Don't let the activity in the other ring or the audience

distract you," Ms. Winters instructed Heather, as if she'd read Liz's thoughts. "You've worked hard for this, Heather."

It was true, Liz noted. Ever since Heather's breakthrough a few weeks ago, when she had finally posted correctly, her entire attitude had changed. Now she was eager for lessons and had become one of those little girls obsessed with horses. *Finally,* Liz thought, *Heather has found something she might be good at.*

Liz just hoped that being forced to compete so early in her training wouldn't set Heather back.

"Where's Mommy?" Heather asked, mounting Mindreader.

"She said she wanted to go change," Liz said.

"Make sure she watches," Heather said, worry creasing her forehead.

"I'm she won't miss it," Liz promised, hoping she was telling the truth.

"Keep your seat, watch your gait, chin up, back straight, elbows in, heels and hands down, and you'll be fine." Ms. Winters patted Heather on the leg. "Off you go."

Heather guided Mindreader to the small ring where the other contestants in her division waited to compete.

Liz watched Heather with affection. *She's really done so well. I hope she wins—or at least doesn't embarrass herself.*

"Tally HO!" a familiar voice hollered. Liz turned.

Dr. Markham-Collins stood in a box at the side of the

ring. She waved her arms to attract Heather's attention.

Dr. M–C had truly outdone herself. A glistening silk top hat with ribbons dangling from it perched crookedly on top of her frizzy curls. Her coat was a bright fire-engine red and taut against her body. Her white jodhpurs stretched tight across her thick legs. Tall black boots completed the ensemble, and Dr. M–C waved her gloves in her right hand and a riding crop in her left for emphasis.

"I'm watching, darling!" Dr. M–C called, her voice startling horses around the arena. "Ride like the wind!"

I shouldn't have worried, Liz thought. *Why would Heather embarrass herself when her mother is so ready to do it for her?*

"Oh, MITZI!" Dr. M–C bellowed to Mrs. Huntington in the next box. "I am SO SORRY that Kelli's mount KNOCKED that jump OVER! You must be DEVAS-TATED that she has been working so hard only to suffer SUCH a DEFEAT."

"Into the ring!" a voice announced. "The level-one walk-trot division."

Liz watched Heather's group enter the ring. Liz spotted little Darien Darrel on a lumbering gray mare ahead of Heather.

"Go, Heather!" Dr. M–C shouted, leaning out from her box and waving her crop in a show of over-the-top enthusiasm. The mothers of the other riders, in neat sweaters and slim pants, stared at her in horrified fascination as she bellowed as if she were at a hockey match.

The girls followed the instructions of the announcer, maneuvering around the ring. Liz caught her breath as Darien had trouble turning her horse around to reverse directions, but Heather seemed to have it all under control. She had a little difficulty when the announcer called for a "sitting trot," but she never lost her cool.

Luckily before Liz passed out from holding her breath for so long, Heather had finished the course. She sat beaming proudly on top of Mindreader as the winners were announced.

"Third place!" Liz gasped when she heard Heather's name announced. "That's amazing!"

"I told you she could do it," Ms. Winters said.

"You did a great job," Liz said. "I never would have guessed she'd get so good. And I've never seen her this confident."

"It's something about riding. I've seen it before," Ms. Winters explained. "She gets to use her natural skills instead of her acquired behaviors. And I just kept telling her if she worked hard, she could do it because she had the talent and the skills. Paid off. Great seat, she has." Ms. Winters smiled. "Give her a treat. She did well."

Heather came out of the back, leading Mindreader by the reins.

"That was fun!" she said. "And look! I got a ribbon."

"I know!" Liz said, giving Heather a hug. "You rode really well. I was so proud of you!"

"Oh, so was I, darling!" Dr. M–C said, stomping up to them. "You made Darien Darrel look like a clod!"

Liz's phone rang and she glanced down. Parker. She felt flutters in her stomach as she picked up. She had no idea how he would act—it had been almost two weeks since they'd last spoken.

"Hey," Parker said. He sounded distant—almost disinterested. "You keep calling me, and I figured I should at least call you back."

"I'm glad you did," Liz said. "Listen, I'm at Madison Square Garden. Heather did really great in her very first horse show, and I am completely thrilled. I want to celebrate. What are you doing?"

"Liz, I'm in no mood to celebrate," Parker said. "You should know that."

Liz took a deep breath. "Parker, I really care about you, and I'm sure you care about me." She spoke quickly so he wouldn't have a chance to contradict her. "Even if you don't want to see me any more as my boyfriend, I still want you to know that I'm your friend. Some of the most fun I've had in the past few months has been with you."

"Liz, look, I—"

Liz cut him off. "Listen, Parker, I'm really happy about

Heather, I'm off, it's a gorgeous day, I want to see you. What do you say?"

"I have no money," he said flatly.

"Since when do they charge for a walk?" Liz demanded.

Parker chuckled. It was the first time Liz had heard him do that since the scandal.

"Come on," Liz urged. "You know you want to."

"Okay," Parker said, his voice sounding warmer. "But just for a little while."

"Thanks, Parker. I'll meet you on Central Park South at Fifty-ninth, near the statue."

"I'll be there," Parker said.

And I need to come up with something fantastic to do! Liz realized. *Fast!*

CHAPTER NINETEEN

high in the sky

Liz hurried to meet Parker. She didn't have time to change, so she hoped she didn't smell like the horse show.

She spotted Parker leaning against the side of the statue. He had his head down, as if he didn't want anyone to notice him.

He looks so . . . defeated, Liz thought. Usually Parker carried himself with confidence and style. Today he slumped against the statue like a kid afraid he'd be picked last for a team.

"Hey," he said as she approached. "So, I made it."

"And I'm really glad," Liz said. Despite the fatigue and obvious worry on his face, Liz thought he looked as handsome as ever.

"So which way?" he asked. "Where do you want to go for this walk?"

"I know a fabulous place with an incredible view. We can have drinks and something to eat there."

Parker's jaw tensed. "You know I can't do that stuff right now. I thought you understood that." He sounded aggravated.

"Hey," Liz said. "Trust me."

"I don't like you treating me, Liz."

"We'll split it," Liz said. "And I promise you that it is cheap. Super cheap. And I can guarantee you've never been anywhere like this before."

Parker gazed at her a moment, then shrugged. "Lead on."

They walked east along Fifty-ninth Street in an uneasy silence. Liz really hoped that her plan wouldn't backfire.

"How are things going?" she asked finally, breaking the silence. She wasn't sure if she should give him space or encourage him to talk. She opted for talking—all the unspoken words between them made her feel too awkward.

"Not so great," Parker admitted.

"Really?" Liz said.

"My dad's out on bail, at least, but he still isn't around much. Mostly he's with the lawyers. The freezing of the accounts is hard. My mom is keeping everything afloat with her own money, but the feds are trying to stop that, too."

"Sounds hard on you," Liz commented.

"It's hard on me because it's hard on them. Well, it's hard on me, too, because my so-called friends have all dropped me. I'm dead to my old posse in New York."

Liz shook her head. She couldn't believe that his friends would drop him just because he was going through hard times. "You're not dead to me," Liz said firmly.

Liz came to a stop on Second Avenue, right under the Queensborough Bridge. Because it was the weekend, traffic wasn't too bad, but it was still a busy intersection. Parker looked at her quizzically.

"So . . . this is it? You wanted to walk to the East River?" he asked.

"You'll see," Liz said. "But first you buy the drinks." She pointed to a hot dog cart at the curb.

"Really?" Parker asked.

"Diet Coke for me," Liz said. "Tell him a cold one from the bottom of the fridge."

"Okay. You're in charge," Parker said.

They strolled up to the cart. The pungent smell of the steaming hot dogs, grilling onions, and hot pretzels made Liz's mouth water.

"A Coke and a Diet Coke," Parker told the short hot dog man. "Cold, and from the bottom of the fridge."

The hot dog man pulled out the sodas, gave them to Parker and took the money. "Anything else?" he asked in a thick Hispanic accent.

"Two bags of Fritos, please," Liz said, holding out three dollar bills.

Transaction completed, Liz slipped her arm through Parker's. "Now for something really special. Time for a ride on the Roosevelt Island tram!"

"Are you serious?" Parker asked.

"As a heart attack," Liz said, leading him into the tram terminal. She pulled out her MetroCard and swiped her fare and pushed through the turnstile. She handed the card back to Parker, who had a confused expression on his face.

"Come on!" Liz urged. "We don't want to miss it."

Shaking his head, Parker swiped the card and walked through the turnstile. They trotted up the stairs to where the tram was waiting. Liz was thrilled to see they were the only ones taking the trip.

"I've never been on this thing," Parker admitted as they stepped into the bright red cable car.

"Adrienne and I sometimes take it over to Roosevelt Island in the summer. It's the cheapest trip out of New York!"

The doors slid shut, and the cable car lurched as it rose high above the East River. Liz stumbled into Parker, who gripped her tightly.

"Maybe we should sit," he said.

"Oh, I don't know," Liz said. "It's kind of like our own little amusement park ride!"

As the tram rose higher, the wind made it sway. "I see what you mean," Parker said, laughing. He strode to the enormous windows and gazed down.

"This view is amazing!" Parker said.

Liz smiled up at Parker. She was happy to see that he was grinning.

"Very fabulous," she agreed. "And over on Roosevelt Island there are all these parks, and even an old, abandoned building we can explore."

"Cool," Parker said. She felt his arms go around her waist and he pulled her into him and kissed her neck. "Though I think I could just ride our private tram back and forth all day."

Liz snuggled closer. "Works for me!"

CHAPTER TWENTY

lock and load

"I knew Graydon and Cam couldn't be up to any good," Liz said. "I *knew* it."

"*I* should have known it," Adrienne wailed. "Why do I always give people the benefit of the doubt?"

Liz and Adrienne sat in Emma's room on Sunday morning—the day of the benefit—working out the details of Adrienne's revenge. Liz had been both horrified and disgusted by the shocking plot between Cameron and Graydon, and she had promised Adrienne she would be on board for anything Adrienne wanted to do.

"Speaking of benefits . . ." Liz looked at Adrienne. "What are you going to do about the Young Lions event?"

"I'm going," Adrienne said firmly.

"Are you kidding me?" Emma shrieked. "I thought you said you went to a school for smart kids. You are so dumb!"

"Actually, Emma, I think you'll approve." Adrienne

shut her eyes and shook her head. "Though I'm being a terrible role model and encouraging all kinds of bad behavior."

"Really?" Emma asked, suddenly interested. "Like what?"

"Do you have Mimi's phone number?" Adrienne asked Liz. "I tried to look it up, but the family is unlisted."

"You need Mimi's number?" Emma asked. "I can get it for you."

"How?" Adrienne asked. "You can't ask Cameron for it. She can't know that I'm going to talk to Mimi."

"She won't," Emma said, turning to her computer keyboard. "I've done this before. It will just take a minute."

"What are you doing?" Liz asked as Emma's hands flew over the keyboard with the same agility she demonstrated at the piano.

"I'm hacking into Cameron's Sidekick," Emma explained. Suddenly the screen went pink, and scores of phone numbers appeared against the background.

"917-PCS-MIMI," said Emma triumphantly. "Thirty-eight seconds. That's a record, even for me."

"You're a wonder," Adrienne said. "I knew you were the perfect ally. Hand me the phone."

Adrienne punched in the numbers and waited for Mimi to answer. She crossed her fingers for luck. Liz and Emma watched her with curiosity.

"Hello?" Mimi answered cautiously. Adrienne figured it must have been because she recognized Cameron's number on caller ID.

"Mimi? This is Adrienne Lewis. You probably don't remember me, but a couple of months ago we had dinner at Khmer with Cameron Warner."

"I don't," Mimi replied, annoyed. "And I don't know how you got this number."

"That's not important," Adrienne said. "What *is* important is that I know that Cameron has been trying to destroy you ever since you won Deb of the Year. I know that she was behind that nasty piece on Page Six, and I know that even now she wants to make sure you are embarrassed at the Young Lions event at the New York Public Library."

"I'm listening," Mimi said. "What's your name again?"

"Adrienne," she replied.

"Right," Mimi said. "The redhead. I remember. The one with the dull boyfriend Cameron turned into a plaything."

"*Ex*-boyfriend." Adrienne winced. She hated that Mimi remembered her as someone Cameron had tromped on.

"What do you want?" Mimi said.

"I want to meet you in an hour to tell you how I'm going to help you stop Cameron."

"It sounds to me like you want to fix Cameron even

more than I do," Mimi said. "Well, okay, I admit I'm curious. But I don't want to meet you in public. Cameron will hear about it. Come to my place. Ten-oh-one Park Avenue."

"Which apartment?" Adrienne asked.

"Oh, please," Mimi said. "Just ask for me at the door." She hung up.

"We're meeting her at her place in one hour," Adrienne announced.

"Adrienne, what are you going to do?" Liz asked.

"I'm going to get Princess Mimi to help me make New York see what pigs Cameron and her brother are." Adrienne sighed. Plotting revenge against Cam and Graydon was the only thing that was keeping her from sobbing into her pillow all day. How she hated that they had used her!

Adrienne turned to Emma. "I may need you to help with some of the technical aspects, since you seem to be so good at spy toys."

"You see," Emma said, "my *CSI* training comes in handy."

The three girls froze at the sound of a knock on the door.

"Adrienne?" Graydon asked from behind the door. "You need a ride home?"

"Here goes nothing," Adrienne murmured, slipping the disks into her bag. "Everyone act normal."

"Stay out, you creep!" Emma shouted.

"Normal, Emma!" Adrienne whispered.

"That *is* normal!" Emma hissed back as the door opened.

"So, you want to take off?" Graydon asked, leaning in the doorway.

"Actually, Liz and I have plans," Adrienne said.

"Getting ready for tonight?" Graydon asked. "I can't wait to show you off to all of New York at the benefit."

"I can't wait to go," Adrienne purred, sidling up to Graydon and letting him wrap his arms around her. *Stay calm,* Adrienne told herself. *Resist the urge to strangle him.*

Graydon leaned in toward Adrienne. "And after the event," he whispered, "I've got a big surprise for you."

"Graydon," Adrienne said, putting as much flirtation into her voice as she could, "I can't believe that anything you could do would surprise me."

"I bet I can!" He smiled, and Adrienne wondered how she had ever seen that grin as anything other than a slimy smirk.

"Liz, see you around. Munchkin," he added, addressing Emma, "you have got to get out more." Graydon grinned and left the room.

Adrienne, Liz, and Emma all looked at one another, then simultaneously mimed gagging.

"Now tell me why you're here," Mimi said, settling into a gilded chair in her vast living room. She picked up a glass of iced tea from the silver tray brought to her by her uniformed butler.

"We have a proposal for you," Adrienne said. She sounded more confident than she felt. Mimi's extraordinary penthouse was extremely intimidating. She was really grateful that Liz had agreed to come with her.

"Just get to the point," Mimi snapped. "I have Frederic Fekkai coming to do my hair in an hour."

Adrienne swallowed and glanced at Liz. Liz gave her a small nod of encouragement. *Well, I've come this far—and it is for Mimi's own good.*

"There's something you need to hear." Adrienne held out a CD.

Mimi looked at the disk disdainfully, but she took it and got up from her chair. She touched a button on a remote control and a large painting of a castle rose on the wall, revealing a hidden stereo system. She slipped in the disk and turned up the volume.

"So, the article went well, huh?" Cameron asked.

"Better than you imagined," Graydon responded. "How great was it that it ran in the same issue as the photos of us reading to those kids?"

"Mimi's such an idiot." Cameron giggled. "She'll never figure out that I was the one who switched the papers and leaked the rumor. Princess she may be, but I think the inbreeding has knocked out a few brain cells. Mimi's not exactly the brightest diamond in the Fallschirm family tiara."

Adrienne glanced at Mimi. Although the princess seemed perfectly composed, Adrienne noticed two bright pink spots high on her normally pale cheeks.

"I'm surprised you asked her to be part of the presentation," Graydon said. "I'd think you'd want all eyes on you. You don't usually like sharing the spotlight."

"I didn't want to have to write that stupid speech about funding and percentages and crap," Cameron said. "Let her be the drone."

"She's going to get up onstage in front of all those people who think she's practically illiterate?" Graydon snickered. "Genius. I wish I'd thought of it."

"This benefit should shove Mousy Mimi off the society pages once and for all."

"Enough," Mimi said, clicking off the CD player. She looked at Liz and Adrienne with new respect. "I don't know how you two got this," she said, "but I'm in. What do you need me to do?"

Adrienne walked to the curb, where the Warner town car sat waiting. The chauffeur opened the door, and Adrienne slipped in, lifting the hem of her Zac Posen dress so that she wouldn't step on it.

"Are you ready for an absolute blast?" Graydon said, leaning in for a kiss.

The only blast I want to see tonight is your plan blowing up in your face, Adrienne thought. She forced herself to kiss him back, knowing that her scheme depended on Graydon believing all was well in Warner-land. *Pretend he's Orlando Bloom,* Adrienne told herself. *Pretend he's Jake Gyllenhaal. Pretend he is anyone else—just don't throw up.*

A few days ago they would have used this time alone in the car for some serious fooling around. Now she hoped she could hold him off till they got there. She really didn't know how well she could pretend to be into him anymore. Fortunately, traffic on Fifth was light, and they soon pulled up in front of the library.

Graydon pulled her a little closer. "I have something for you." He reached into his pocket.

"Tonight's a big night for us," he said, looking deep into her eyes. Adrienne wanted to Taser him. "We should celebrate in a very special way." He pressed a key into her hand. "This is for the Royal Suite at the Waldorf-Astoria—for when the party's over."

"Wow," Adrienne said, fighting the competing urges to laugh and to deck him. "You think of everything, Graydon. That is so special."

"No, you're the one who is special," Graydon said. "So different from the other girls."

Right. So different, you think it's cute to humiliate me just to amuse yourself and Cameron. Luckily, her hurt and shame had been completely taken over by anger, and she didn't feel the urge to cry—just the determination to make sure he got what was coming to him.

Graydon helped Adrienne out of the car and took her hand. The long, wide steps to the library were covered with a red carpet and votive candles. The cameras flashed as they ascended the stairs, and the socialites around them smiled at the paparazzi.

They reached the top of the stairs, and Adrienne peered inside the historic, majestic New York Public Library.

The white marble gleamed in the Astor-Lenox-Tilden Hall, and the gilded names of library donors carved into the walls sparkled in the party lighting. Enormous floral arrangements stood on either side of the doors, and more flowers were draped along the molding like garlands. Gorgeous people in elegant gowns and handsome tuxes chatted animatedly in groups.

What a pretty setting, Adrienne thought, looking up at Graydon, *for such an ugly scam.*

CHAPTER TWENTY-ONE

the center of attention

Liz gripped Parker's hand as they stood on Forty-second Street and waited for the light to change. The imposing white library building seemed strangely ominous to her. Maybe it was the special lighting that made it shimmer ghostlike in the spring night. *Or maybe I'm just worried about what's going to happen tonight,* she thought. *To Parker, to Adrienne, to everybody.*

Parker had the cab drop them off on the opposite side of the street so that no one would see that he wasn't arriving in a limo. Unlike the rest of the guests tonight, he had only two transportation options: subway or taxi.

Parker stared across Fifth Avenue. Photographers were snapping pictures and shouting out the names of the celebrities and society people attending the benefit.

"Oh, man," he murmured. "The vultures are out in force tonight."

"Do you think the other entrance will be open?" Liz asked.

"What other entrance?" Parker asked.

"On the Forty-second Street side," Liz explained. "When I did research here, I got out of the subway right next to a side door."

"Good thinking," Parker said. He gave her hand a squeeze.

Liz squeezed back. She was really glad she had been able to talk Parker into attending the benefit. She wanted him to see that his life wasn't over just because of his dad's problems.

They crossed Forty-second Street and hurried toward the narrow stairs which led to the side entrance.

"You were so smart to remember this entrance," Parker said. "It's really—"

"PARKER! PARKER!" a dozen voices shouted at once, as the paparazzi leaped from behind the bushes where they were hiding, their cameras exploding with flashes. Liz suddenly saw the world as if it were lit by a strobe light.

"Is your dad innocent?" one reporter shouted.

"Will you visit him in jail?" shouted another.

"How does it feel to be poor?" shouted a third.

Liz felt Parker freeze. "Come on!" she urged. She yanked him through the crowd toward the door.

A library security guard stepped outside and prevented the reporters from entering the building. It gave Parker and Liz a chance to slip into the foyer.

"Wow, buddy," the guard said after he had locked the side entrance. "You famous?"

"Sort of," Parker said. "Is there another door out of here?"

"Parker, come on," Liz coaxed. "We're here. Let's go upstairs and have fun."

Parker sighed. "All right," he said. "I give up. Let's go."

They showed the invitation to the guard and then climbed the steps to the main entry hall of the library.

Liz gasped.

The chandeliers were dimmed, and the hall was decorated with dozens of fully grown birch trees, their branches hung with tiny votive candles that flickered in the dim light. Thousands of trailing strands fell from the trees, some a few tiny inches, others grazing the floor. As Liz approached one of the trees, she realized that the strands were composed of thousands of rose petals threaded onto silk cords.

"I can't believe it," Liz said. "It's all so beautiful."

"*You* are beautiful," Parker said. "*That* I'll admit."

Liz flushed with pleasure. "Well, I guess that's the most important."

Luckily, because of Graydon's position as co-chair of the Benefit Committee, he had a lot of meeting, greeting, and handshaking to do. That meant Adrienne just had to plaster a big fake smile on her face and not cringe if he touched her. That was easier than having to talk to him, or worse, flirt and kiss.

Butterflies were break dancing in Adrienne's stomach and she wasn't sure if it was nerves or Graydon making her want to barf. Was her plan going to work—or was it going to backfire horribly?

Graydon slid his arm around Adrienne. "Did I tell you how gorgeous you look in that dress?" he said.

Adrienne glanced down at the sea green gown she was wearing. The intricate seaming formed leaf patterns across the bodice of the dress, and pale beige fur trimmed the scooped neckline. The color set off her red hair beautifully, and the slim fit showed off her tiny waist.

Her shoulders sagged as she remembered how excited she had been when she had tried on the dress, how much she had looked forward to coming to the benefit as Graydon's date. Back then, she'd thought tonight would be memorable as the night she'd take her place in front of all of Graydon's society friends as the girl he loved. Instead, she was just some toy mouse he and Cameron were batting around between them for amusement—like a pair of nasty cats.

Graydon nuzzled the back of her neck and she flinched. She felt him pull away, startled. Recovering quickly, she said, "That tickles!" She forced herself to giggle.

Graydon picked up a champagne flute from a waiter's passing tray. "Drink?"

"No thanks," Adrienne said. She needed every one of her brain cells tonight. *Where is Liz? It would be a lot easier to manage Graydon's groping if she were here with me.*

Adrienne finally caught sight of Liz coming into the main hall with Parker. Liz looked drop-dead gorgeous in a striking midnight blue Armani—bought on super-sale at the legendary Loehmann's. But even at 75 percent off, it must have put a serious dent in her college fund. Parker looked every inch the sophisticate in his black tie—a junior James Bond. But both of them looked a bit strained.

"Well, Parker's either got serious stones, or he's a flaming fool," Graydon said.

"What do you mean?" Adrienne asked.

"Showing up tonight," Graydon explained. "*Everyone* in the city is here. Including most of the gossip columnists and society editors in New York."

"Good," Adrienne said. Graydon looked at her sharply.

"I mean, that's cool." Adrienne smiled sweetly. "It shows what an important event this is with you and Cam as co-chairs."

"Hey, there," Liz said, walking up to them. Parker looked around, anxiously trying to gauge people's responses to him. Adrienne glanced around, too. A few kids were staring, but most were just into snacking on the tiny hors d'oeuvres and talking. *Maybe tonight won't be so hard for Parker after all,* she thought. *That will be a big relief for Liz.*

"Hi, Liz, hey, Parker," Graydon said. "Um, Adrienne, we should get our seats."

Adrienne glanced up at him. He seemed eager to get away from Parker, as if Parker's family problems were contagious. *What a jerk,* Adrienne thought. *They'd been pals all through prep school. Then again, why am I surprised that Graydon has no sense of loyalty?*

"Well, well," said a voice behind Adrienne. "Is a charity giving away free tickets to this event now?"

Graydon stepped aside, and Cameron joined the group.

She looked incredible, as always. Her hair was pulled straight back, and she was wearing a long white Gucci dress that hugged her body.

"So, Cameron," Adrienne said, quickly changing the subject. She knew Cameron's dig was aimed at Liz and Parker. "It must be exciting to be presenting tonight."

"Yes," Cameron replied. "It's wonderful to have been blessed with so much money, and to be able to uphold the family reputation by doing charitable works." Cameron looked pointedly at Parker, who squirmed under her unspoken criticism.

"Well," Liz said brightly, "we'll see you all upstairs."

No! Adrienne's brain screamed. *Don't leave me alone*

with these two! But after Cameron's snide remark to Parker, she knew there was no way he and Liz were going to hang out with them.

The butterflies in Adrienne's stomach turned into bats as she climbed the stairs with Graydon and Cameron to the Main Reading Room. Adrienne's green eyes widened as they entered. The room was breathtaking.

The long reading tables with their brass standing lamps had been transformed into long banquet tables covered with linen and gold-banded china. The lamps had shades made of garlands of rose petals, and the scent of flowers filled the room. The soft lights flattered everyone, even the figures on the incredible ceiling murals.

"Quite romantic, don't you think?" Graydon said to Adrienne. "The perfect prelude for our special night."

She bit the insides of her cheeks to keep from blurting out a barrage of insults.

Cameron's icy eyes flicked from Graydon to Adrienne. "Is that true?" she asked. "Will you and Graydon be going somewhere tonight? Like *all the way?*" She snickered.

I know where you two are going—straight to hell! Adrienne thought.

"Well?" Cameron pressed.

"We're going to get to know each other . . . *better*," Graydon said. He pulled Adrienne in closer. "Isn't that right?"

"He's absolutely right, Cameron," Adrienne said. "I'm getting to know the *real* him." *And what a real slimeball he is.*

"Oh, Gray," Cameron said. "We just have to go say hello to the Huntingtons." She slipped her arm through Graydon's. "You understand, don't you, Adrienne? Family only."

"Gee, Cameron," Adrienne said, "I feel like I've been learning all about how to be a Warner." *And you're about to find out what a quick study I am.*

"You'll be fine on your own, Adrienne," Graydon said.

"Yes," Cameron added, "I'd hate to have to explain that my brother is actually dating the help."

Cameron and Graydon strolled through the crowd, heads together, talking and laughing. *Probably congratulating themselves on how amusing their little bet is turning out to be,* she thought. *Just you wait.*

Adrienne felt a freezing cold hand on her back. She spun around and saw Mimi behind her. She quickly turned back so that it would look as if they weren't speaking. Adrienne pulled a DVD out of her evening bag and passed it to Mimi, who immediately disappeared into the crowd.

Here we go, Adrienne thought.

Soon everyone was sitting in their seats, and Adrienne found her spot with Cameron and Graydon right up front.

"James Brightlock," said the man on Adrienne's right, "Allied Capital."

"Adrienne Lewis," she replied, shaking his hand, "Van Rensselaer High."

Mr. Brightlock laughed and turned to Graydon. "Gray, how's your dad? He must be very proud of you two."

"Oh, he *is*," Cameron gushed.

Mr. Brightlock craned his head around. "Where is he? I'd love to talk to him about this new investment I'm very excited about."

"Oh, he couldn't make it," Cameron said airily. "He'd rather be the genius *behind* the scenes. He hates fuss."

He'd rather stay home and drink, you mean, Adrienne thought, though she was surprised that *Mrs.* Warner wasn't here. She thrived in these social settings.

As if she'd read her mind, Cameron continued, "And Christine just couldn't bear to leave his side. They're just so cute together."

"Besides," Graydon added, "this is really Cameron's night to shine."

Ahhhhh, that's it, Adrienne thought. Christine probably desperately wanted to be here, and Cameron nixed it because she didn't want to share the spotlight.

To her surprise, Adrienne was actually relieved to hear that Christine wasn't going to be there to witness the humiliation awaiting Cameron and Graydon. The COW was selfish, vain, self-centered, and a royal pain, but she wasn't actually cruel. She didn't deserve to have to deal with the drama of the Warner kids going down in flames.

She can read all about it on Page Six tomorrow. Adrienne smirked. *And then the fireworks will really begin for Cameron and Graydon.*

"Oh, look, it's starting," Mr. Brightlock said, as Mimi took the podium at the far end of the room. "I'm surprised to see Miss von Fallschirm up there."

"Oh, that was my idea," Cameron announced. "I just thought it would be good for her to share a little of my joy. After the whole scandal, she was just devastated. But I feel it's important to face up to the terrible mistakes you've made."

Mr. Brightlock wasn't the only person at the benefit surprised to see Mimi. A low murmur circulated through the crowd.

"Good evening, everyone," Mimi said. Her voice could barely be heard, despite the microphone.

Poor Mimi, Adrienne thought. *Everyone at this event thinks she's dumb AND a cheat. She's got a lot of courage.* Adrienne didn't think she could stand up there in front of all these people knowing they thought the worst of her.

She could see Mimi tremble a bit—though she wasn't sure if it was from nerves or anger at how Cameron had totally trashed her reputation.

"Oh, poor thing," Cameron said gleefully. "She sounds so nervous and unsure of herself. She really should never have been made Deb of the Year. You need much more poise and self-confidence to handle all the responsibilities."

"Someone like you," Graydon said.

Cameron lowered her eyes demurely. "Well, I would never say that. . . ."

Adrienne fought the urge to smack Cameron. Instead, she focused on her plan. She gave Mimi what she hoped was an encouraging smile. *The truth will come out soon,* she thought.

Mimi must have understood, because she nodded back and cleared her throat. "Welcome to the Young Lions of the New York Public Library Benefit." She sounded more confident.

Good, Adrienne thought. *Keep thinking about the payoff.*

"Cameron Warner has graciously invited me to tell you about the Warner family's many contributions to the library, and all the good the foundation has done over the years."

Mimi launched into a long speech filled with facts and figures about donations, growing the endowment, communities served, and philanthropic trends. She even ran a PowerPoint program with graphs and pie charts.

Adrienne's eyes began to glaze over. *No wonder Cameron wanted Mimi to present this portion of the program,* Adrienne realized. *Cam wouldn't want to do the boring bit, much less do the research!*

As dull as Mimi's presentation was, it was the key to

the success of the plan to expose Cameron and Graydon as the nasty little monsters they were. It gave Mimi and Adrienne access to the audiovisual equipment. And Emma's techno-savvy made sure their DVD would work.

Mimi stopped the program running the slides on an image of the Warner Foundation logo. "Now, it's my honor to introduce our next speakers, the co-chairs of the Young Lions Committee for Development, Cameron and Graydon Warner."

Everyone applauded, and Cameron and Graydon swept to the stage. When the girls met for an air-kiss at the podium, they were so far apart, Adrienne couldn't believe they had bothered.

"Thank you all so much," Cameron said, flanked by Graydon at the podium. "And let's all give Mimi a round of applause." Cameron beamed at the crowd, straight into the flashing cameras. Graydon stood beside her looking smug. "Now, I won't take long," Cameron said. "I know after Mimi's speech the *last* thing you want is to sit through a boring presentation. But don't worry—*ours* is cool!"

Graydon leaned into the microphone. Cameron looked slightly peeved, but he spoke, anyway. "We want to thank the library for allowing us to use this event to make this very exciting announcement. Our family's foundation has decided to create a new organization with a brand-new grant: The Little Lions, a remedial reading class for children."

The audience applauded obediently.

"Anyway"—Cameron crowded Graydon away from the microphone—"we have a video presentation to explain more about our project. So please start the DVD." Cameron turned to face the large screen.

Sappy music began to play, and the faces of adorable children staring at books filled the screen. Cameron's voice was heard.

"Children?" she screeched. "I don't give a flying crap whether or not the urchins can read! Maids don't need to read, do they?"

"I know," Graydon said. "What a waste of time. You looked great in that picture, though, reading to those poor kids. You looked almost like you cared."

Cameron snickered. "I cared about how my hair looked."

A shocked gasp filled the room. Cameron frowned and stared up at the screen. "That's not what it's supposed to say."

The volume on the sound track went up even higher. "That trick you played on Mimi was brilliant," Graydon's voice continued.

"It was so easy to switch her essay with the one I wrote," Cameron said. "And those gossip writers are such bottom-feeders that they couldn't wait to snap up the humiliating news."

Adrienne noticed the Page Six reporter pause mid-scribble, an infuriated expression on her face. Then the woman wrote twice as quickly.

Onstage, Graydon and Cameron tried to grasp what was happening. "Someone changed the audio!" Graydon exclaimed.

"But how did they—who would—" Cameron sputtered.

Cameron flushed a deep scarlet and raced from the stage, covering her face with her hands as photographers snapped pictures in a frenzy.

"Turn that off!" Graydon shouted from the podium. "And whoever did this is fired!"

Adrienne grinned, enjoying every minute of the humiliation.

"I said turn that damn thing off!" Graydon yelled.

The audio track went silent. In fact, the entire room went silent. Then everyone began talking at once.

CHAPTER TWENTY-TWO

mission accomplished

Liz watched Cameron and Graydon flee past her table. "Gee, looks like they're in a big hurry," she said to Parker. "Isn't it rude for the hosts to leave before the guests?"

"Well, you know Cam and Gray," Parker said. "They've always lived by their own rules."

"Hopefully now they won't be able to get away with so much." Liz shivered. "I can't even imagine being so mean."

Parker nodded. "This was low even for him."

Everyone around them was talking about the scandalous revelations about the children of one of the most prominent families in New York. The buzz was practically deafening.

"At least now everyone will be gossiping about someone else for a while," Parker said. "This should knock my family off the gossip pages for at least a day or two."

"That should be a relief," Liz said.

"Yeah . . ." Parker's voice trailed off as he looked around the room. Then his blue eyes focused on Liz. "Liz, I—I owe you an apology."

"You do?"

"I've been giving you a really hard time. And you never, ever deserved it."

Liz shrugged casually, but she flushed a bit, knowing that Parker was really making an effort; that he understood a little of what it had been like for her. "You were going through something really intense," she said. She gazed down at her lap, not wanting him to see the emotions flickering across her face.

He raised her chin up. "Yeah, that's true. And all you ever did was try to help. I see that now."

Liz took in a deep breath. For some reason his nice words were threatening to make her cry.

"Like tonight," he said, leaning back in the chair and surveying the room. "I *so* did *not* want to come. But now that I'm here, I'm glad you forced me."

"Yeah?" Liz asked, looking up at him.

"Not everyone here is treating me like dirt," Parker said. "Maybe there are some people in this town who are able to see past all this glitter and drama and actually behave like friends."

"You see!" Liz said. "Welcome to the real world, Parker."

Parker grinned. "I only said *maybe*. I haven't actually decided if my theory is true or not."

Liz shook her head, laughing. "Well, at least it's a start!"

"You know," Mimi said, coming up from behind Adrienne, "I really owe you for this one."

Adrienne smiled and turned to face Mimi. "I'd say we both contributed to tonight's success. After all, I had my own reasons to want to out Graydon and Cameron as the evil duo. Maybe now they'll stop."

"Let's hope so," Mimi said. "Cameron has been trying to make me look bad for years. She's so jealous that I'm a princess, because it's something she can never be. She'll do just about anything to make me look dreadful. It's wearisome."

"If you're a princess, does that mean your father is a king?" Adrienne asked.

Mimi smiled patiently. "No," she replied. "It just means that once, very long ago, our family ruled a very small part of a piece of land that became part of Austria."

"When?" Adrienne asked. "Like, in the eighteenth century?" She was studying that period in her history class.

"No," Mimi said, "like, in the ninth."

Adrienne smiled. "Seems like a long time to hold up a reputation."

"Believe me, it is."

"Speaking of reputations, I'm going to go salvage mine," Adrienne said. "I'm going to find Graydon."

"Good luck," Mimi said. She moved through the crowd, head high. Adrienne was glad to see the swarm of guests who hadn't been very welcoming at the beginning of the evening stopping to talk to her.

Now if I were a pair of humiliated, spoiled brats, where would I be? Adrienne wondered. *Trying to get to my limo!*

Adrienne scurried down the hall to the doors. She spotted Cameron and Graydon huddled by a column. They looked as if they were trying to become invisible. Luckily for them, everyone was still upstairs, gossiping about what had just happened.

Adrienne smiled and walked up to them.

"Leaving so soon?" she asked.

Graydon looked at her, pained. Cameron stared past her as if she weren't there.

"I think you two owe a lot of people apologies," Adrienne said.

"We'll never apologize to you," Cameron snapped.

"I wouldn't expect you to," Adrienne said. "The way you treated Parker—that was really shameful. I hope you two learn a lesson from how you both get treated in the next few weeks."

"If I *ever* figure out how you did this," Cameron said, "I will get even with you."

"How, Cam?" Adrienne asked. "Will you ruin my reputation?"

"You don't even have a reputation," Cameron said. "You're already nothing in this town."

"I'm really sick of your threats," Adrienne said. "And guess what? After tonight, my reputation trumps yours any day!"

Cameron shot Adrienne a withering stare, but then crumpled. She leaned against the pillar and shut her eyes, as if she believed that if she couldn't see anyone, no one could see her.

"Oh, and Graydon?" Adrienne said. "Just so you're clear? I was onto your little bet all along. I was just playing with you to see how far you would take it."

"Sure you were, nanny," Graydon scoffed.

"I guess you'll never know for sure, will you?" Adrienne taunted. "And you know what—I wonder what would happen to your success as a ladies' man if it got around that you couldn't even make time with the high-school nanny."

"Shut up," Graydon snapped.

"Oooh, clever," Adrienne said.

Cameron's eyes popped open. "You are so fired."

"I don't think so," Adrienne said. "How happy do you think Christine is going to be when she hears how you two trashed the family? After all her hard work to try to make the Warners respectable? She is definitely not going to fire me on *your* say-so."

"I said shut up!" Graydon shouted.

"Who knows? This could even get you cut out of the family fortune all together." Adrienne doubted this was true, but she was on such a role, she couldn't bear to stop.

At those words, Cameron and Graydon both looked stricken. Cameron's already pale complexion went ashen, and Graydon's mouth hung open.

Graydon's cell beeped, indicating that his driver had arrived at the library. Graydon snapped open his phone. "Side entrance," he ordered. "Now!"

"Ta-ta!" Adrienne called, as Graydon and Cameron raced down the hall.

She pulled her cell out of her tiny evening purse. "Emma," she said when the little girl answered, "you did great. Mission accomplished!"

Liz stepped into the ladies' room. She and Parker had found a quiet corner and kissed all of her lipstick off. She wanted to freshen her makeup in case any of the photographers snapped her.

She stood at the sink and applied the deep rose lipstick when Adrienne burst into the room.

"We did it!" Adrienne squealed. She threw her arms around Liz, and together they jumped up and down.

They pulled apart and grinned at each other.

"Congratulations!" Liz said. "You really pulled it off. And those two really had it coming. "

"Amazing." Adrienne burst into giddy peals of laughter. "You know, I felt a little guilty at first about embarrassing them that way. But when I realized how many people they were hurting—"

"Total no-brainer," Liz said firmly. "It was the right thing to do."

"I need to get Emma a *big* present," Adrienne said. "But what do you give the girl who has everything? Literally!"

"You know, Parker's dad knows lots of TV people," Liz said. "Maybe Parker can set up a visit to the *CSI-New York* set."

Adrienne's eyes widened. "Brilliant! That is the best." She gave Liz another hug, then stepped back. "So how *is* Parker?"

Liz smiled a slow, satisfied smile.

"I know that look," Adrienne said. "Your plan worked. He's actually handling real life!"

Liz nodded. "I think he's really beginning to get it. At least he's willing to give it a shot."

"That is so great!"

Liz looked at her friend in the mirror. "How are you *really*? I mean, I know you're totally psyched over what just happened, but you were so into—"

Adrienne cut her off. "Don't even say his name."

"So . . . are you okay?"

Liz watched Adrienne swallow hard. "I'm still getting used to it," Adrienne admitted. "But it's not like I'm mooning over him—wishing we could get back together. You know what? Red-hot anger takes away a lot of the heartache."

"That's good," Liz said.

"And I really am glad that things are working out with Parker," Adrienne said.

Liz shrugged. "For now. He's pretty unpredictable. In another week, I could be as single as you are now!"

"You know, Liz," Adrienne said, as the two friends walked arm and arm back into the library, "I've been thinking . . ."

"About what?" Liz asked.

Adrienne sighed. "Well, since the whole Graydon thing blew up, I've realized that I'm happy with my friends, with my family—at least most of the time—and with school. What makes me *really* unhappy is being around the Warners. So . . ."

"So what?" Liz asked, her eyes widening.

"So, I'm going to quit working for the Warners."

"No!" Liz said.

"Yes." Adrienne said firmly. "I'd rather work at a Dairy

Queen than go into that snake trap again."

"What about Emma?"

"Emma will be fine without me. She's smarter than all the adults in her life," Adrienne said.

"You know that the COW will just offer you more money, and you'll cave," Liz teased.

"No way. Not this time," Adrienne said. "I'm a whole lot better person than they are. I'm worth too much to sell myself for so little."

"You know," Liz said, "you're awfully smart."

"I know." Adrienne grinned. "So are you except for this babysitting hang-up you have. If it weren't for that, we could go into business together."

"Design shoes," Liz said.

"Hand-paint furniture," Adrienne responded.

"Mix lip glosses," Liz countered.

"We could do anything, together." Adrienne smiled. "Come on, Liz, you know you're too good for them."

"I wish I could," Liz said, "but I just like Heather and David way too much to leave . . . just yet."

"Soon. Soon," Adrienne predicted.

"Who knows?" Liz said. "But now I'm going to race you to the dance floor. The DJ is really hot tonight!"